Table of Co

Gia: Outcasts MC Book 1

By Mel Pate

Copyright page

· · · ·

· · · ·

authormelpate@gmail.com

Chapter 1

Gia

As I stand in the dimly lit room with the faint scent of sweat all around me, my anticipation for the fight builds.

My long hair is tightly French braided, and now Big C is wrapping my hands in preparation for the match.

This ritual is comfortable for us with the number of times we have repeated this process. As he is taping my hands, I get myself in the right headspace to kick some ass.

The distant sounds of the crowd, the rhythmic chants, and cheers reverberate through the warehouse walls that hold the underground fights.

"Keep those hands up, Gia," Big C's voice breaks through my thoughts—his words laced with worry.

Not that I would lose, but that I would be injured.

"And watch out, she's a southpaw," he glances up from my hands to ensure I'm listening to him.

I nod. My focus becomes sharper with each passing moment. Southpaws are a different breed. Their stance is opposite ours, so it's off-putting to many fighters.

The anticipation builds like a crescendo. Just as Big C finishes, I hear the sound of the bell ringing.

My turn, I think, as I start bouncing and shadowboxing again to keep my muscles warm and loose.

I roll my shoulders and head, then ask through my mouthpiece, "What's the payout so far?"

"It was up to 15 grand when I came back here. But stop thinking about the money and concentrate on the fight. You have three rounds to knock her out."

I nodded and bit down on my mouthpiece. My determination set to get the entire amount.

I hear my nickname being called over the bullhorn to announce me to everyone. Big C holds his fists out, and I bump them, then turn towards the door.

We stepped out of the small room into the smoke-filled hallway with people eyeing us. Bo, my best friend, has been with me since my sophomore year of high school, falls into step behind us.

I keep shadowboxing as we walk by people trying to talk to me, but all I can hear is my heartbeat in my ears and the roar of music.

As we step into the light, I focus on the ring. With each step of our approach, the cheers grow louder. "Rebel, Rebel, Rebel."

Hearing my nickname cheered is a feeling like no other.

Tonight's energy is palpable as I make my way ringside.

Big C lifts the rope for me, and I climb into the ring. When I stand up straight again, a rush runs through my veins. It's welcoming, like an old friend.

I square myself up and lock eyes with my opponent tonight. A silent vow passed between us to inflict pain and knock the other out.

The referee's voice cuts through the roaring noise over the bullhorn, signaling everyone to quiet down.

Without hesitation, I step forward, and so does Iron Maiden, my opponent.

Iron Maiden is not to be taken lightly. At 5 foot 10 inches and at least 40 pounds heavier than me, she looks like a Viking with her flaming red hair and an all-muscle athletic build.

Being a southpaw will be a challenge, and watching her past MMA bouts, she's tough as hell. I'm unsure what she's doing here fighting tonight, but it's not my business.

It's a good thing I was trained hard in both martial arts and hand-to-hand growing up.

The ref takes her hands in his first, examining them. "A kill shot gets you banned. No weapons, no chemicals. Anything else goes."

Then he grabs my hands and does the same examination, but my eyes never leave hers.

I'm 5 foot 8 inches and weigh 130 lbs. She is larger by a good amount. But you know what they say. The bigger they are, the harder they fall. She could take me in an MMA match with all the rules, but in the underground, it's my turf.

I block those thoughts out and concentrate.

Wear her down with headshots and kicks, then go for the body till she opens herself up for a knockout, I tell myself, ignoring the ref as he keeps talking.

The pressure is on her. I'm undefeated, and I'm sure she wants me out of the way bad enough to make a mistake or two.

"Three rounds, Gia, knock her out," Big C shouts as I return to my corner. I nod so he knows I heard him.

"I hope your bets are placed because the fight starts now!" The ref yells into the bullhorn and steps back against the ropes, handing it off to another man over the side.

Without hesitation, I spring into action. Meeting Iron Maiden in the center as she runs at me. She is preparing to do what she's known for: the flying knee.

As soon as her feet leave the ground, I drop low, sliding, grabbing her extended back leg. Jerking it, making her face plant.

I immediately go for the Americana, an arm lock submission. She flips and rolls us and lands a solid strike to my side; pain radiates through my ribs, letting me know I'll need to get them checked later.

Just as I see her eyes flicker, I swing, and the sound of my fist meeting her flesh seems to echo as we each unleash a barrage of strikes.

Each of her blows seems to be fueled by sheer determination. Mine are more calculated. One hit to the face for every two to her abdomen.

She is fighting back with equal ferocity, but I can block most of them.

Her assault is solely MMA moves. Doesn't she realize she is limiting herself? I pushed harder. With each strike, I became more precise to break through her defenses.

I see her setting up for an axe kick, and I rush her, going low and tight, picking her up and body-slamming her.

The air whooshing from her body is unmistakable.

I quickly came down on her full-force elbow to the solar plexus. She curls into a ball double in half from the pain.

But that's not what I want. I need a KO.

I jumped up. I motion for her to get up and come at me. I was taunting her in front of the crowd.

It fuels her, and she gets up swinging. The crowd's roar is growing more distant with each blow we trade. As I throw a solid hit, splitting her eyebrow, I feel the pain go through my side again.

The telltale sign she landed a solid blow to my ribs. I press forward with even more determination as the bell rings, ending round one.

We each back away slowly to our respective corners to prepare for the next round.

Big C removes my mouthpiece so I can rinse my mouth, and I see his lips moving, but I can't hear the words.

I'm too focused, and the cheering is deafening.

The bell signals the start of round two, and I turn my eyes locked on Iron Maiden. She is going down is my only thought right now.

As I approached the ring's center, she launched forward with renewed ferocity as her fists unleashed a barrage of strikes. She is trying to end this quickly.

Her movements are fueling mine. I met her blow for blow as I watched for my opening.

Once I see it, I pivot my foot and jump, unleashing a roundhouse kick. It connects perfectly with the side of Iron Maiden's head.

The sound is unmistakable, and I know she is going down.

Time seemed to stand still as she staggered sideways; her eyes glazed over as she crumpled to the mat.

The crowd erupted into cheers as the referee pointed for me to go to my corner.

He counted down from 10, but she was out cold.

The ref approached me, grasping my wrist and raising it, declaring me the victor.

I spit my mouthpiece out along with blood just as Big C entered the ring, coming to my side with a wide grin. His smile was contagious, making my own show an appearance.

Iron Maiden's coach knelt beside her as she started coming around. I walked over, ignoring the ref's protest. He should know by now how I am.

I stand over her and outstretched my arm and hand, offering it. My opponents may be obstacles to me during a fight, but we are all people afterward.

I'll give respect where it is due. She fought a good fight, one of the better ones I've gone up against.

She looks at my hand, then looks back up to me, taking it. I pull her up to a standing position and grin.

"You're tough as nails red. Good fight."

She turns her head, spitting her mouthpiece out, then grins at me.

"They don't exaggerate when they talk about you. How about next time we have a few drinks before we go at it?"

"Deal," I reply, laughing, walking back to Big C.

As we made our way towards the hallway, my eyes caught sight of a group of men I had seen many times at these illegal fights.

They are military or vets by their demeanor and stance. You can't miss their MC cuts in this crowd, either. But the one on the left catches my attention. He's a little older than the rest, his arms crossed over his chest with bulging biceps. I've never seen him before.

The hair on my arms stands up, and my skin tingles. Our eyes locked, and I couldn't help but smile at him. He returned it as I walked past. Damn, he's hot.

Once we were back in our room, it wasn't long before the doctor arrived. Thanks to Big C and Bo demanding he come immediately.

He examined me carefully after I lay down on the bench near the wall. A split lip and some bruising are nothing. Then he started poking and prodding below my sports bra.

"I would say you have two cracked ribs, young lady, but there's no way to be sure without x-rays," he eyes me carefully.

"Do you want me to wrap them?" he asks, knowing this isn't my first rodeo with fractured ribs.

"If you don't mind," I smile at him but wince from the sting of my split lip.

"I'll prepare the wraps if you want to rinse off in the shower." I nod and grab my bag, going into the small makeshift shower—no hot water as usual.

I quickly wash my body, leaving my hair braided. Then throw on jeans and an old band T-shirt.

After the Doc wraps my ribs tight, Big C, Bo, and I collect our winnings and make our way to his pickup.

Once we arrive back at the gym, I take the envelope out and divide the money in half.

"No, Gia, that's too much," he says, holding his hands up to refuse it.

"I'm out for the next month with cracked ribs, plus I have something big happening soon. Take the money for the kids and foodbank. Put what you need towards utilities. You know as well as I do the kids need us and the gym. Do it for them," I tell him, knowing he won't refuse.

Once he takes it, I turn towards Bo, who has been quietly watching.

"Ready to call it a night?" he grins.

6

"Hell yes," I reply, hooking my arm with his. We walk around the side of the gym and start up the stairs.

I pull my key out once we reach the top, unlocking the door to our upstairs apartment.

When I announced last year that I was moving out after a massive fight with my parents, they flipped and tried to get me to either stay or take one of the penthouse suites in one of the hotels my family owns.

To me, that was just another way for them to control me. So, when Big C offered for me to move into the empty apartment above his gym, I didn't hesitate.

No one knows except Bo that I will be moving even further away soon if everything goes as I plan.

I drop my bag on the floor in the living room and sit on the couch to remove my boots.

"You did good tonight, princess," Bo says, making my head jerk in his direction. His lip quirks up in amusement.

"You must not want your cut calling me that." I raise an eyebrow at him.

His hands go up in surrender. "Just joking."

I stand, walk over to my bag, and remove the envelope. I count out two thousand, handing it to Bo. "Thanks for having my back."

"I always do and always will," he replies, taking the money. "What time is your birthday dinner tomorrow?" he asks.

I groan at the thought of going to my parent's estate. It will just be another fight, and we all know it. "5 pm is what Mamma said when she called yesterday," I reply.

Bo nods but gives me a sympathetic look. "I'll be ready. And by that, I mean for anything." He quirks an eyebrow.

I smile and walk over to him, giving him the hug, he deserves. "Good night, Bo," I say. Walking to my room, I run my fingers across one of the maps pinned to the dining room wall. "Soon," I whisper.

Right now, I need to rest before I have to deal with my family tomorrow. Happy birthday to me.

Chapter 2

Blaze

I take a long swig of my beer while I listen to Cowboy, my V.P., and Axel, my Enforcer, giving Hawk a hard time over his upcoming fight tonight at the underground warehouse.

I usually don't go to these fights unless one of us will fight. With Hawk climbing into the ring, I know it is a guaranteed payout. He's a hot head on a good day, which is common with redheads. But in a fight, he's a beast. I'll definitely be placing a bet.

"Rumor has it tonight's Rebel's last fight," Cowboy says, leaning back in his chair. That catches my attention. The guys are constantly talking about a female fighter named Rebel. According to them, she's not just beautiful but can handle herself.

"Where did you hear that?" Axel says, sitting his beer on the table and leaning forward with interest.

"Overheard the same dude that's always with her at the fights telling Big C," Cowboy replies.

"When was this?" Axel asks.

"When I was at the gym last Monday working out," Cowboy says.

"Damn, if it's true, I'm definitely putting a bet on her tonight then. Fighters always want to go out with a win. Bet she is fierce in the ring tonight," Axel says with a cocky smirk.

"You coming, Pres?" Cowboy asks, looking at me.

"Ya, I'm not missing out on watching Hawk go kick someone's ass in the ring. Besides, I could use some extra cash," I reply, looking around my bar.

Things have been slow in Angel's for the past two weeks now. That means our cash flow is low for the club and cash in my pocket.

I raise my hand and motion for Hunter and Kane, who are at the bar flirting with two chicks from the city trying to get laid to get over here.

Once they approach our table, I give them a don't argue with me look. "I need you two here tonight running the bar. If anyone gives you shit, handle it," I say.

"You got it, Pres," They reply in unison.

Thirty minutes later, the rest of us mounted our bikes to go to the warehouse. Pulling onto the road, I look to my left at the empty building where my pop's gym used to be and shake my head.

I was deployed overseas deep in the shit when Jose and Raphel came into Freedom with their drugs and prostitutes taking over. They terrorized the residents, scaring the neighborhood kids and smashing windows or robbing the businesses that wouldn't pay up for protection or give them a cut of their profits.

In less than a year, they ran off all the residents, and the businesses closed up shop, moving elsewhere. Leaving the small town, I grew up in deserted except for them and their little enterprise.

Raphel has taken up shop in the old abandoned Grand Hotel with his hookers, and Jose set up a drug distribution center out of the only apartment complex in town. His runners into the city, and his young dealers live in the apartments.

My anger surges, remembering that I wasn't here to help pop. When my term was up, I didn't reenlist. There are too many demons in my head after the last deployment after things went to shit for our unit. It was time for me to come home. But home wasn't what I found. What I came back to made me feel sick.

Pop wanted me to take over the new location in Wells City he opened and run it. But that wasn't for me. I'm not the same man now that I was when I enlisted. Society doesn't understand what you see or how it changes you. I don't belong in society or agree with their rules. Neither do the rest of the Outcasts. That's why we decided to form the club. We operate by our own rules and moral code.

Once we reach the warehouse, we all park and dismount. Looking around the parking lot at all the vehicles, they have one hell of a turnout here tonight.

Axel falls into step beside me as we enter with Hawk, Kane, and Thor right behind us. We go up to register Hawk for his fight, and the man holding the clipboard nods at Hawk, recognizing him.

"Hey Hawk. You signing up?" He asks.

"Ya, who you got to put me against tonight?" Hawk asks him.

"Got a new guy from out of state that looks challenging. Says he's undefeated up North," he answers with a grin.

"Put him in with me, and I'll change that for him," Hawk shoots back and cracks his knuckles.

"What are the odds I'll place my bet now," I say, then laugh.

"With Hawk," he pauses, eyeing Hawk, then looks back to me. "The best I can do is 1 to 3."

I nod in understanding and reach into my wallet, pulling out the $500 cash I have on me. It's not a great return, but it's a profit. There's no doubt Hawk will win, and they know he will, too.

I hand it to him, and he gives me the clipboard to sign.

We all make our way to the far wall next to the hallway that leads to the fighter rooms. None of the guys ever use them. They just remove their shirts and boots before entering the ring.

Part of being a member of the Outcasts MC is always being ready for a fight. I make damn sure they are, or they never make it past prospect. Hell, most don't even make it to prospect.

Leaning against the wall, I watch three matches while I alternate, scanning the room for possible problems. It's an old habit. One that I will gladly keep, especially with the Diablo's so close to us. Who the fuck calls themselves the devils? I shake my head. Their territory and clubhouse maybe 100 miles away, but they have been seen twice in the last month getting close to our territory.

They are known to take young women to turn them out and always look for new routes to run guns. It won't be happening in Freedom. Especially after I finally make my move and get rid of Jose and Raphel.

Hawk's name is called over the bull horn, and he sheds his shirt and boots, marching towards the ring. We follow in step behind him to stand ringside.

The Northerner who bragged about his rep at signup lasted 3 minutes into round 1 before he was out for the count. I chuckle and shake my head.

After collecting my winnings, I retake my spot, leaning against the wall by the hallway with my arms crossed over my chest. It isn't long before two names are called out. The first is Iron Maiden. A tall woman with an athletic build and red hair exits the hallway beside me, making her way to the ring. As she walks away, Hawk whistles and catcalls her, but she ignores him.

The next name called is Rebel. It's almost instant that the chanting starts. "Rebel, Rebel."

I turn my head and see my Pops exiting the hallway with the most beautiful woman I have ever seen. My heart starts pounding hard against my ribcage as my eyes rake over her.

Her dark hair is tightly braided, but I can tell it's long. She has Olive skin and dark eyes with long lashes. My eyes go lower. Big round globes are spilling over the top of her black sports bra. As she passes, my eyes glance down to her thick thighs and lush ass.

I reach down, adjusting myself at the thought of pounding into her. What the hell? A woman hasn't piqued my interest in over a year.

A blonde man follows closely behind her, scanning everyone like he is protecting her. Boyfriend? Fuck that. If he is anything other than a bodyguard or friend of hers, I'll have to teach him differently. That woman is going to be mine.

"You ok, Blaze?" Cowboy yells into my ear and squeezes my shoulder.

I realize my hands are balled into fists, and my body is rigid.

"Ya, I'm good. What's her name?" I yell back.

"I've heard them call her both Rebel and Gia at the gym, so take your pick," he replies.

I nod so he knows I heard him over the crowd. My eyes never leave her as the ref checks their taped hands and talks to each of them.

When the bell sounds, I can't hear anything over the roar of chatter and yelling at Rebel and Iron Maiden. When the fight starts, they immediately meet in the middle and start fighting.

Fuck my dick is at full mass watching her go at it in the ring. They've both had some training. Iron Maiden mainly sticks to MMA moves, but Rebel uses different techniques. Has she had some hand-to-hand or combat training?

The first-round ends, and I watch Pop talk to her, but she either isn't listening or can't hear him. She is in her own head right now.

I step forward and watch closely when the bell rings for round two. Rebel is calculating and waiting for her moment. When Iron Maiden least expected it, Rebel got her with a roundhouse to the head.

"Shit, that had to hurt," Cowboy yells out.

I chuckle. "Hell, I think Maiden was out before she hit the mat," I reply.

What happens next surprises me. When the ref releases Rebel's hand, declaring her the victor, she walks over and offers a hand up to Iron Maiden.

I don't think I've ever seen a fighter do that. "She has good character," I murmur to myself.

When they exit the ring, pop gives me a slight nod, gesturing for me to come back to the room, but I shake my head. I know he wants me in his life more, but my demons are too dark. It's best if I stay away.

All thoughts fade from my head when Rebel gets close. Her eyes roam over my body. Then I see lust in her eyes. Hell yes, baby, look all you want. When her eyes meet mine, I give her an easy smile. We will definitely be talking soon. When she returns my smile, I feel my heart pounding.

Shit, I need to find out more about her. Now is not the time to approach her. "But soon, very soon, you will be hearing from me," I say as she walks out of sight.

I hear laughing and turn, seeing the guys all looking at me. Fuck, how much of that did I say out loud?

"Mind your business and collect your money if you placed a bet. We're heading out," I say gruffly.

As a few guys head up front, I turn to Cowboy. "I need to know everything you can find out about Rebel or Gia. Whatever the fuck her name is."

His smile grows. "You got it, Pres."

Fuck me, I'm never going to hear the end of this. Women always throw themselves at us. Me, in particular, being the President of the MC. They want to be an old lady or brag that they have ridden one of us.

A few of the guys will take up the offers from the women who come by the bar from the city. I want no part of it. One-night stands aren't for me.

Once we return to the bar, Cowboy gets us all drinks while we sit at our table in the back. Only the original seven founding members of the Outcasts are allowed to sit here.

It isn't long before Cowboy makes it back with a round of beers for us, but Hunter rolls up in his wheelchair beside him.

"Cowboy said you wanted the 411 on Rebel," Hunter eyes me but has a cocky smirk on his face.

I ignore it because I need to know what he has. "Tell me everything you know," I say firmly.

"Her real name is Gia, but most call her Rebel. She is the one who started the foodbank and youth center in the back of your Pops gym. Rumor has it that she has a soft spot for teenagers from rough homes or poor neighborhoods. She keeps them off the streets, out of trouble, and makes sure they have something to eat. Even helps some with homework after school if they need it," Hunter says, and I know my face shows surprise.

I had heard from pops a few times in passing how a woman had worked miracles with some local kids and had been helping him with the gym, but I wasn't listening too closely. Shit, it's her.

"Do you know a last name, where she lives or works?" I ask.

"Not many know personal details about her. All I can tell you is she spends most of her time at Big C's and has been staying in the upstairs apartment with the guy you saw tonight. I think his name is Bo," Hunter says.

As soon as the words leave his mouth, I slam my beer on the table and clench my jaw.

"Who is he to her?" I spit out with venom.

"Don't know exactly, but in public, they act like brother and sister or best friends. They've never acted romantic that anyone has talked about," he replies.

I relax a little at that. But there is no way they are related. They look nothing alike. Bo is light-skinned and has blonde hair. She has dark hair, tan skin, and the most beautiful brown eyes I have ever seen.

I nod in thanks to Hunter, and he rolls back over to the bar.

"You going to see her?" Cowboy asks me over his beer bottle.

"Ya, soon," I reply, giving nothing else away. Soon, my little Rebel, you and I will get to know each other.

Chapter 3

Gia

The hot spray of the shower flows over me, and I take a deep breath, trying to relax my muscles. Pain rips through my left side, and I brace myself against the wall. Ok, no deep breaths or raising my left arm for a few days.

I tilt my head back, wetting my long hair as my mind drifts to the kids at the youth center. Spending the day with them will cheer me up before I go to the birthday dinner my family has planned.

I was clear with Mamma that I only wanted a quiet dinner with family. I lay my forehead against the tile shower wall, and my gut tightens with dread. When have they ever paid attention to anything I wanted?

Quickly but carefully washing my hair and body, I get out to dry off. I find a simple black tank and my favorite jeans with a rip in the knee.

After doing my morning routine and getting dressed, I walk out of my bedroom into the kitchen. Bo is sitting at the bar drinking his morning coffee.

"Morning," he grumbles, making me laugh. He is no more a morning person than I am.

"Morning Bo. You coming to Big C's with me?"

"Ya, someone has to keep you out of trouble," he smirks, setting his coffee down. "How's the ribs?"

"As long as I don't breathe deeply or raise my arm too high, they're fine," I reply, pouring myself a cup.

"Just work with the kids to keep your mind busy. If anything happens tonight, we'll leave. I have your back," Bo says, standing and, in 2 long strides, has me in his arms.

"Thank you for being my person," I mumble into his big chest.

"You're mine too, you know," he replies, kissing my forehead.

"Always am, always will be," I tilt my head, grinning at him. Throwing the exact words back at him, he always tells me.

He chuckles and shakes his head at my antics.

We go downstairs, and it is already busy.

I had forgotten about Big C running a free three-day public trial to get new memberships.

I see 2 of my kids by the punching bags and smile. One holds the bag while the other goes through combinations, hitting it. I am so proud of them now.

We only have five kids here regularly. 4 teenage boys, the oldest is 17, and one girl, Mia, is 17.

They all have troubled pasts. Coming from low-income families or just being from the wrong side of town set them up for being bullied in school. Or worse, selling drugs for dealers. Hell, after I started bringing them to the gym with me to work off the anger they carried inside, I found out a few of them didn't have enough food at home.

After talking Big C into letting Bo and I turn the back Storage room into a food pantry with healthy snacks, bottled water, and soup, we set it up fast.

They now have a safe place to do their homework, work out their anger in the gym or ring, and eat when hungry, no questions asked.

I have bonded with them over the past two years. There may only be a four years difference between me and the oldest among them, but in some ways, I feel like their guardian watching over them.

I see Mia at the speed bag, building a good rhythm. She is so focused on what she is doing that I startle her when I speak.

"Nice job. Everything OK?" I ask her, now realizing she wasn't just focused. Mia's eyes look tired, like she hasn't slept, and her face is red. It's too red for just using a speed bag. She's pissed.

"Ya, I'm fine," she replies, giving me a fake smile. I know that smile. She doesn't want to talk, just hit something. I understand that feeling.

"I'm here if you need me," I say firmly, raising my eyebrow so she knows I'm serious. She gives me a nod and goes back to hitting the bag.

If her father is back to drinking and hitting her again, I won't hold back this time. I warned him a year ago after Mia entered the gym with handprints on her arm and a black eye. If he ever touched her again, I would teach him a lesson he would never forget, and I meant it.

Mia has been through enough growing up without a mother because of a drunk driver. She then had to practically raise herself because her father started drinking and becoming violent.

None of it makes sense. Nothing in life makes sense to me, but it will. I'll give myself a couple of days for the pain to ease in my ribs, and then I'm going to put my plan into action.

I walk towards the weight room where Bo is, and I see a man who looks familiar. He is all over a blonde pushed up against the wall.

I stop 5 feet away as the rank smell of alcohol wafts towards me. Their hands are all over each other, and he is grinding his hips into her.

Who the hell comes to the gym reeking of alcohol, especially at 10 am?

The man kisses down the blonde woman's neck and buries his face in her breasts. "Damn baby, you have a great rack," he says in a thick Italian accent, groping her.

That's when it hits me. I know him, it's Lorenzo Bianchi.

I look over at Bo, who has paused, mid-curl with a barbell, watching them too. I raise an eyebrow in question if he recognizes him also. His slight nod lets me know he does.

I ignore them and grab a stack of dirty towels, taking them into the back to launder. If I can't work out, I'll clean up.

The hours must have flown by. I'm in the ring holding mitts up for TL to practice his combinations when Bo approaches the ring. "Time to call it quits and celebrate," he says, leaning on the ropes.

I glance up at the clock on the wall, seeing it's after 5 pm. Shit, I drop the mitts and go to the locker room to shower and change back into my street clothes.

Is it normal to dread your birthday or to see your family? After showering, I quickly dress and just let my hair air dry. I'm sure I will get plenty of crap about my appearance from Mamma and Papa, no matter what I wear or look like.

They wanted a boy, but when they got me, they wanted a princess. Dresses, makeup, parties, and someone papa could control and sell off into marriage, strengthening family ties. I guess nothing worked out in their favor; I laugh to myself.

I throw my dirty gym clothes in a basket before walking out. As soon as I step through the doorway, I jump in surprise. Big C, Bo, and my kids are waiting for me, yelling, "Happy Birthday!"

I grab my chest and laugh. "Thank you."

Big C walks up, handing me a cupcake with a lit candle. "I hope whatever you wish for comes true, darlin'. If anyone deserves a wish, it's you."

Shit, he's going to make me cry. I close my eyes and wish for everything to go smoothly when I attack Jose and Raphel, and then I blow the candle out with a smile.

The kids rush me in a group hug, crushing my tender ribs. I grit my teeth because it's worth it. They bring me happiness. We stand talking and each eating a cupcake until Bo reminds me it's time to go, ruining the moment.

Bo is waiting for me by the door, so I hook my arm through his and lay my head on his bicep as we walk outside to our bikes.

"Happy birthday, Gia," Bo says warmly, placing his hand over mine on his arm.

"Thanks, Bo. Maybe we can get a drink and celebrate after this dinner?" I ask.

"Anything for you. It's your day, after all," he replies.

As our bikes roar up to the iron gates of my family's estate, the guard opens them on our approach. I nod as we ride past, following the concrete drive to the main house.

When the mansion comes into view, I feel rage boil up inside me. This isn't the quiet family dinner I agreed to. This is an all-out party, D'Angelo style.

There are limos and town cars parked everywhere. The backyard and garden are full of wives, children, and men from different families my father does business with. My eyes travel further, seeing guards and foot soldiers walking the grounds in large groups, armed patrolling.

I snap my head to Bo, who just turned his bike off and lowered the kickstand. "Want to just leave now?" He asks, dead serious.

"No, I'm not leaving yet. Knowing my father, he has done this with a plan in mind. If it's the same thing, he pulled on my 20th, trying to marry me off and thinking I'll be embarrassed enough by all the people here to accept he's wrong. I'll make him out to be the fool. I'm sick of this shit and sick of how they treat me," I spit out with venom.

Removing my helmet, I slam it onto the seat after I stand. They want to pull this shit on me. I'm ready for it. I'm fed up with trying to win their love that should be given freely or biting my tongue to keep some semblance of peace. It all stops now.

Bo falls into step as I take long strides around the house towards the backyard. If I go through the house, Mamma or Papa will try to corner me with threats to behave and play along. That's not going to happen.

Once we make it around the house, I immediately spot a bar set up and go straight for it. A stiff drink in my hand will make this go smoother.

The young woman bartending smiles at my approach. "What can I get you?"

"Jack and coke, make it a double," I say, placing my hand on the bar, but my eyes never stop roaming the crowd. I haven't been noticed yet, but it won't take long.

Bo orders a beer, no doubt wanting to stay sober to have my back. He steps closer, throwing an arm over my shoulders.

"How are you going to play this?" he asks, taking a drink of his beer.

"Like any woman would, that's fed up with people's shit. I'm letting my inner bitch out," I say with a grin.

"Fuck, ok then let's do it," he replies.

I put my arm around his waist and go to a table set up with dinnerware near the house. It is separated from the others, letting me know where Papa and Mamma intend our family to sit. He always has to stand out and be better or higher than anyone.

I go right to the center of it, facing all the other tables, and sit with a smile like I'm the damn queen of the world. Bo takes the seat next to me and leans back, appearing relaxed. I know better. His body may say comfortable, but his eyes say he's ready to hurt someone at a moment's notice.

Chapter 4

Bo

I sit back in my chair next to Gia, stretching my legs out beneath the table, and throw my arm over the back of her seat. I take a drink of beer as my eyes scan the crowd.

"Looks like Papa couldn't resist making a spectacle," Gia murmured.

My jaw clenched at her words. I thought my family was the worst for kicking me out, but her family is disgusting. No matter what she does, they put her down. Her clothes aren't appropriate, her hair's a mess, and a woman in her 20s should be married to be beneficial. Since when does getting married and popping out babies define if a woman is of use?

I guess it's an Italian thing, or maybe it's mafia. Fuck that shit. Gia is an amazing person. She is my family now. I glance at her, and my gut clenches. Tonight, isn't going to end well, but I'll be here for her just like always.

Her body stiffens, and she sits her glass down. I follow her line of sight and see her father's imposing figure cutting a path through the crowd with her mother at his side.

He stops a few feet from the table and stares down at Gia. "Gianna, I thought we raised you to have some manners. You arrive yet don't come into the house to greet your Mamma and I?" He makes a point to speak loud enough for everyone to hear, and my fist clenches.

Gia puts on a fake smile. "Hello, Papa. It made more sense for me to come out here since you invited all these guests. Doesn't a good host entertain guests that arrive at a party?" Gia says back, and I have to bite back a laugh.

Her father's eyes narrow, and his face reddens. Her mother visibly squeezes his arm to calm him.

"Gianna, why don't you help me in the kitchen before the food is served?" Her mother asks with a worried look on her face.

"Mamma, we both know the staff doesn't need help in the kitchen," Gia pauses and tilts her head to the side. "I think you want to chastise me for how I spoke to Papa, or maybe you want to warn me about what this party is really about."

Oh fuck, Gia isn't mixing her words tonight. I take a long drink of my beer and lean a little closer to her. Her father doesn't miss my movement. When his eyes land on me, he scowls.

He has never liked me. Gia says it's because I'm not Italian, and my sexual preferences bother him. But it's more than that. I think he hates anyone supporting her and encouraging her to be strong. He wants all the control.

At Gia's words, her mother gasps, covering her mouth like what she said was vulgar.

"Gianna, you will not speak that way to your Mamma," her father growls out, and everyone near us goes quiet, watching the scene.

Gia takes a drink and then sits her glass down. "I'm sorry, Papa, I forgot you don't like hearing the truth. So where is this food? I'm starved," she says with a grin, changing the subject.

Everyone sits, but the mood is uncomfortable. When Lorenzo Bianchi and his father approached the table sitting directly across from us, I realized Gia was right.

"Gianna, it's wonderful to see you," Lorenzo says with a smirk.

"I wish I could say the same," Gia spits back, and I can't hold back my chuckle.

"Gianna, you will not speak that way to your guests," her father yells, slamming his fist on the table, and the music stops.

"Papa, I didn't invite them. You did technically; that makes them your guests. Why don't you tell us all why you really threw this big party? We both know you didn't do it for my benefit," her voice raises with each word.

I hear gasps and chatter, and her father stands, slamming both hands on the table and making his chair fall backward. He raises his

23

hand, pointing at her. "This is your engagement party. You will be marrying Lorenzo Bianchi next month." His eyes are cold, and his voice is stern.

Gia calmly reaches for her drink, but I know she isn't calm inside. I'm sure her heart is breaking right now.

"You want me to marry a man who less than 12 hours ago was dry-humping a blonde in public, complementing her nice rack of tits, and practically motorboating her in a room for everyone to see?" she asks him, and I nearly choke on my own spit.

Her father's head snaps to Lorenzo with a death glare. Lorenzo just laughs along with his father.

Gia stands just as I see her Nonno exit the house a few feet away, walking in our direction. Gia walks over, standing directly in front of her father, and I stand behind her.

"Papa, I will never enter into an arranged marriage. Not for you or anyone else. A daughter is not a commodity to be sold like a piece of meat. They are supposed to be loved. But you wouldn't know anything about that now, would you?" she jets her chin out in defiance, watching him.

"How dare you disrespect me like this, and how dare you accuse me of not loving you?" he bit back, grabbing her arm roughly.

That's it. I step to her side, but Gia gives me a look, letting me know she will handle it. I don't like this shit at all.

"When have you ever taken an interest in my life? Came to one of my fights? Stopped by the youth center I run? Hell, even asked me how my day has been?" she raises an eyebrow at him.

Her father is vibrating with anger now, and he pulls on her, trying to take her to the house, but she jerks her arm from his grasp.

"No, Papa. You wanted to do this in front of a crowd. Let's finish it here," she yells, planting her feet firmly and squaring her shoulders.

"You first have to know someone to love them. Secondly, those words have never passed your lips with my name in my lifetime. Third, the damn trust fund you so often threaten with never giving me if I don't do as you order. Well, you can stick it. From this moment forward, you are no longer my Papa. Not that you have ever been one. Stay out of my life, and I'll stay out of yours," she says firmly, but I can see the tears welling up in her eyes.

To my shock, her father raises his hand in the air to strike her. As I throw my hand in front of Gia to push her out of the way, her Nonno grabs his son's wrist.

"You have made a complete fool of yourself, son. I am ashamed of the way you have treated my granddaughter. If you or anyone else attempts to bring harm to her in any way, they will be dealing with me. Am I understood?" Her Nonno bellows out loudly, but his eyes flash in warning.

"Si," Gia's father grits out between clenched teeth. When her Nonno releases him, his eyes bore into Gia with pure hatred.

"You are no longer my daughter and no longer welcome here. Get out before I have you removed," her father's words are cold, and I know they cut Gia deeply. But this will all be for the best. Her parents have never shown her love.

I take her hand, and we walk around the house back to our bikes with our fingers laced together. "Are you ok to ride?" I ask her as she picks up her helmet.

"I'll be fine as soon as I get out of here," she says as her hands visibly shake. She gets frustrated with the strap, slings her helmet across the concrete driveway, and mounts her bike.

No helmets, then, ok. I walk to mine and straddle it. Before we start the engines, her Nonno comes into view, walking towards us.

When he approaches, he doesn't stop until his arms are around Gia. She buried her face in his chest, inhaling deeply like a child would.

"I will stop by tomorrow. You and I have much to discuss," he tells Gia softly as he strokes her long hair.

Gia raises her head and smiles at him, but her eyes are full of tears. "I love you, Nonno."

"Ti amo piccola ragazza," (I love you, baby girl) he replies with a smile.

When he steps away, we start our engines and ride side by side out of Hell's gates. That's precisely what this place has always been for Gia. Now, she is finally leaving it for the last time.

Once we make it through the city, Gia rolls the throttle, opening her bike up. Her long dark hair is flowing behind her in the wind like a cape. I do the same, staying at her side.

We go under the overpass for the Interstate, and I know where she is leading us: Freedom. We both slow down and cruise through the old town when we arrive at the town line.

Empty, run-down buildings with busted windows line the streets. We pass the old grocery store and gas station, slowly taking everything in. Nothing has changed since last week.

Gia heads to the far end of town where the old Grand Hotel sits. It's nothing more than a brothel now, but it won't be for long. Slowing as we approach, there is loud music blaring from inside and trash all over the parking lot that has six vehicles parked in it.

We make a wide circle and head back in the direction we came in.

A couple of miles before we reach the overpass again, I see Angel's. It's a bar that opened two months ago. According to Big C, his son is the president of the Outcasts MC and opened it after returning from the military.

Gia looks at me, jerking her head toward the bar, and I nod. If she wants to drink her pain away, I'm here for it.

We pull in and park at the side of the building. The front is lined with bikes, but we should keep ours out of sight for now.

I dismount, waiting for Gia to join me. "You, ok?" I ask.

"Ya, it's over now. I just want to move on," she says with a pain-filled face.

"Time heals all wounds, blah blah blah," I reply, and she laughs.

"Let's get a drink and relax. I need to end this day with some fun," she grins, and I throw my arm over her shoulders.

"Come on, birthday girl, let's start the party," I chuckle.

We walk through the big wooden door to a jukebox playing old rock n roll, a smoke-filled room filled with tables and chairs, and a long bar sits against the left wall.

I guide her to the bar, where she sits and smooths her hair down from the ride.

I sit on the stool beside her and watch the bartender approach. He is in his mid-20s with a prospect cut on. "What'll have?" he asks.

"Jack and coke for me if you have it. If not, a beer is fine," Gia says. He grins wide at her knowingly. I'm guessing he has seen her fight at some point. I've seen their cuts many times at the underground warehouse.

"Sure thing, Rebel. What about you?" He finally looks my way.

"I'll take a beer and directions to the bathroom," I reply.

He taps the bar twice with a nod. "Bathrooms that way," he points to the back corner with a hallway.

"Thanks, man," I say, then look to Gia. "Be right back."

"Don't forget to spit when you're done," she says, then laughs.

Fuck, she is never going to let me live that down. We took off one weekend when we were 18 camping. After a 12-pack, I was buzzed and needed to take a leak. I walked behind a tree and took care of business, but she saw me spit afterward. I chuckle at the memory.

When I come out of the bathroom, a couple of guys are around her. No surprise there. I sit beside her and listen while I drink my beer.

My eyes roam the bar stopping on a member of the Outcasts that's hot as fuck sitting a few seats down with a woman hanging on his arm. She is talking animatedly to him, but his eyes are on me.

He has short dark hair, toned, defined muscles, a goatee, and eyes that are haunted. His square jawline flexes as his eyes roam me with appreciation. My dick jerks when our eyes lock again.

However, that feeling disappeared when he quickly turned his gaze away. Is he in denial? Still in the closet? I reach down, adjusting myself before redirecting my attention back to Gia.

"Is it true you're done fighting?" the man with Cowboy on his cut asks her.

"I hope so, but you never know," she replies. I know she was counting on her trust to carry us through her plan, but now we'll have to find another way.

The man who has been quiet while the others talk finally speaks up. His cut says, President and Blaze. But according to Big C, his son is the president. I can't remember his damn name, though.

"What's your name beautiful?" His eyes are studying Gia, but there is lust lacing his words. Fuck he wants her.

I look at Gia, and her cheeks flush pink. "Gia," she replies, taking a sip of her drink. "What's yours?" she asks.

"Blaze," he replies. "You work at the Gym with my Pops, I hear."

Gia's face shows surprise. Shit, I thought she knew this was Big C's son. "Yes, I help out some. Big C is your Papa?"

"Ya, but we aren't as close as we used to be," he says, looking away.

Gia tilts her head to the side but doesn't question him further about him.

When Blaze looks back, his next question has me sitting straighter. "Where's your family from?" he asks her.

Fuck this is not the day or time to be bringing them up. She needs to forget tonight.

"I'm from Wells City," she says, not elaborating on family, and he catches it.

"What's your last name?" he pushes further, leaning forward.

Gia straightens her shoulders, knowing how people react when they find out who she is or her family.

"It's D'Angelo," she says the words like they leave a bad taste in her mouth.

Blaze and the other two men stiffen. "So, you're the mafia princess everyone talks about?"

My hands are balled into fists as soon as the words leave his mouth. Gia stands and turns towards me. To my surprise, she doesn't say we're going. She asks for change for the jukebox, ignoring what Blaze said.

I stand, reach into my pocket, pull out a handful, and give it to her. But I can see the pain in her eyes again. When she walks away, I whirl on Blaze and his minions.

"I don't give a fuck what you have heard or what you think. I know exactly who that amazing woman is. You know nothing. So, before you start running your mouth, take the time to get to know someone before judging them based on gossip. She's been through enough, especially today of all days," I growl out.

Blaze jumps to his feet, and I'm ready to throw down if necessary. Instead, Cowboy grabs his shoulder, stopping him.

"Think Blaze. You touch him, and you can kiss your shot with her goodbye. Is it worth it?" he asks Blaze.

Blaze looks at me carefully and then nods.

Gia's phone rings on the bar where she laid it, and I glance up, seeing her still at the jukebox. I picked up the phone, saw Big C's name, and answered. "Hey, Big C, what's up?"

His shaky voice and words chill me to my core. "You and Gia need to get here fast. Mia just came stumbling in, beat all to hell. She won't talk to me or let me help her. She's asking for Gia," He rushes out.

I immediately stand up, gripping the phone, and look across the room to Gia. "How bad is she?" is my only question.

"It looks bad, but who knows until she's cleaned up and checked out," Big C replies.

"Fuck, we're on our way," I say, hitting the end call button. I look back towards Gia as I gather our things. "Hey, Gia, we gotta roll out. Trouble at Big C's, and he needs us now."

She whirls around, eyes wide with concern, and starts my way with long, determined strides.

"What's going on?" She asks.

"Mia came in beat to hell and won't talk or let anyone touch her until you get there. Big C is freaking out. Says she looks bad," I explain.

Gia's eyes focus on me, and that deadly look she gets in the ring takes over her face. She turns towards the door, and I take off after her.

Once outside, Gia and I are on our bikes in no time, starting the engines. What surprises me is seeing Blaze and a group of Outcasts doing the same.

Chapter 5

· · · ·

Gia

I rush out of the bar, pulling my key from my jeans. I shove it into the ignition as I straddle my bike, barely noticing Bo doing the same.

Adrenaline and rage are coursing through my veins while images of Mia being seriously injured are playing in my head.

She has to be ok, and once I make sure of that; I'm going to deal with her father or whoever dared to hurt her.

My bike fishtails as I get on the throttle hard, pulling onto the road and riding towards Wells City.

Bo speeds up beside me, trying to keep up. The cool night air whips around me, but it does nothing to dull the throbbing of my ribs. I ignore everything; my only focus needs to be getting to Mia.

The roar of multiple other motorcycles approaching behind us gets my attention. It must be the Outcasts. Shit, hearing there is trouble at his Pops place must have Blaze as rattled as I feel.

As Cruz's gym comes into view, our tires screech as we hit our brakes and cut into the dimly lit parking lot. Once I bring my bike to a sudden halt, my heart begins pounding in my chest.

I throw a quick glance over my shoulder to Bo as I dismount. He is right with me as the roar of motorcycles comes flying into the parking lot, hot on our tails.

I rush to the door, jerking it open with force, sending pain shooting through my side. "Mia," I call out with urgency, rushing inside.

"We're back here," Big C's deep voice rings out through the gym. It came from the direction of the back room, so Bo and I rushed in that direction. Once I step inside, I see Mia huddled against the wall, tightly holding her legs to her chest. Blood stains are on her clothes, and her face shows both pain and embarrassment.

31

Shit, she has nothing to be embarrassed of. I walk over and kneel in front of her. "You look worse than I do after a fight, sweetie. Can I take a look and see how bad it is?" I ask her, trying to get her to relax some.

Her eyes jerk above my head, no doubt seeing Bo and a bunch of bikers. She turns her head from us, not wanting anyone to see her like this.

"Hey," I say, cupping her chin gently and turning her face to look at me. "No judgment from anyone here. We've all been busted up before."

She nods, and I see her shoulders visibly relax and her arms holding her knees to her chest.

"Good. Now, can I take a look and see if you need a doctor?" I ask softly.

"You can look, but no doctors; they're useless," she says with determination and a fire in her eyes. I know she blames the doctor for not saving her mother when she was little. But some people just can't be saved.

"Ok," I whisper, knowing I'll have to convince her to see one if she is hurt badly. "Tell me where you hurt."

My sweet Mia raises her hands, covering her face that is already swelling from being punched, then lowers them to her stomach, lifting the front of her shirt.

Bile rises into my mouth, seeing dark half circles from a boot, no doubt. Someone was kicking her. I raise my hand and gently glide my fingertips over them. When I get to her ribs, she flinches, and I pull my hand away. "You may have some broken ribs, Mia," I say, looking at her tear-filled eyes.

"You function just fine when yours are hurt, and so can I," she choked out, and my heart clenched.

"Just because I do things doesn't mean you should, sweetie," I reply.

Clearing my throat, I continue looking her over and see handprints on her upper arms. My eyes jerk up to hers as I run my hands over the large bruises forming. "Who?" is the question burning inside me.

32

"Padre," (father) she says as tears flow down her cheeks. I hear a growl behind me but ignore it. "I went to bed early so I could help Big C set up for the younger kids tomorrow morning. That's how he got the jump on me," she says, and I feel white-hot rage run through me. The son of a bitch attacked her while she was sleeping.

An outcast I hadn't seen before steps close and kneels beside me. "Mia, my name is Kane. I am a trained S.O.C.M. or a Special Operations Combat Medic. I know you don't like doctors, but I can examine you and help if you'll let me," Kane says in a deep but calm voice.

Another loud growl rumbles behind me, and I turn, seeing Cowboy hovering over us. His whole body is rigid, and he is flexing his fists at his side. Damn, what's up with him.

I glance at Blaze, and his face shows humor watching his V.P., ready to lose his shit.

"You can look and help, but no hospitals and no doctors," Mia says, getting my attention back to her.

I look at Big C, who has been watching over us, and he nods, knowing what I'm thinking. Take her up to the apartment. Put her in my bed. I'll be back within the hour," I say, standing.

Mia looks at me with concern. Shit, I know she doesn't want me to leave, but I can't let this go. "How long till your 18th birthday?" I ask her.

"It's the 3rd of next month," she replies.

"You're not going back there. Your home is with me until you choose otherwise," I state with finality. Her face shows relief, and a pain-filled smile comes across her face, showing blood on her teeth from the busted lip he gave her.

"Thank you, Gia," she says.

"No need to thank me. I've always thought of you as my sister. Now you will be," I say with a nod and turn, marching for the door. The bastard was warned, and now he has to pay.

"Gia!" I heard Mia's sweet voice yell my name just as I was at the door. I turn slowly, looking at her.

"Just don't kill him. I don't know if I could live with that," her left eye is almost swollen shut now, and my heart is breaking trying to see things from her point of view.

I nod. "That's all I'll promise. Your Padre will still be breathing when I walk away. Nothing more." I turn and march outside with determination, hearing multiple other boots hitting the ground behind me.

When I mount my bike, I see Bo getting on his as well as Blaze and three others I don't know their names. It doesn't matter to me as long as they stay out of my way.

I nod to Bo, and he nods back as we start the engines and roar out of the parking lot.

My bike screams beneath me as I run through the gears, winding my baby out. The Texas night air feels thick as we pull onto Mia's street at our destination. I cut the engine and barely get the kickstand down before marching towards the old run-down house.

Bo is calling my name as I hear other bikes pulling to a stop, but I ignore him. My boots make the old wooden porch creak as I step onto it with quick strides and rear back, kicking the door with all my might.

The door flies open, and the frame pulls loose from the wall with the force of my anger. Scanning the disgusting living room, I step inside and feel Bo step up behind me. There is trash, empty food containers, and beer bottles everywhere. "Oh shit, oh shit," comes from the right, and I see a bird in a cage bobbing its head and screeching.

Shit, this is no place for anyone to live. I spot her Padre slumped in an armchair, half asleep, with a bottle of whiskey clutched in his hand.

"Get up!" I yell, my voice full of venom as I advance on him. "You sorry excuse of a man, I said get up!" I grab a handful of his hair in both hands and drag him out of the chair.

The bottle crashes to the floor, and he looks up with blurry eyes and anger. His lips curl into a sneer. "What the hell do you want, Gia?" he slurs out with the rotten stench of whiskey wafting off him.

I fist both hands at my sides. "You know damn well why I'm here. I warned you to keep your filthy hands off of Mia, didn't I?" I cock my head to the side, waiting for his pathetic response.

His laughter catches me off guard, and fury erupts inside me like a volcano letting loose. Without a word, I swiftly lift my right leg kicking him under the chin and sending him flying backward on his ass. "Kick his ass, Kick his ass!" The bird yells in the background.

Blood spurts from Mia's Padre's mouth, and he yells in pain. "Awe, did you bite your tongue? Let me help you with that," I say as I lift my leg again and deliver three hard kicks to his ribs that have him curling into a ball on the floor.

"You're a pathetic piece of shit," Bo growls out from beside me. I turn to him and smile. He always has my back and is always at my side.

"Stand him up for me, please," I say with an evil grin.

Bo smiles down at me and winks. He bends, picking him up for me, and I step close. I want him to see my eyes before I knock him out.

He tries to fight against Bo's hold but is too drunk to do much.

I get my face within inches of his, almost gagging at how bad he smells. "You will look the other way if you see Mia on the street. You will never say her name or try to contact her. Hell, if you even think of her and I find out about it, there won't be enough of you left to give the earthworms a snack. Do. You. Understand. Me?" I spit every word with force, so he gets the gravity of what I'm saying.

His eyes go wide when the realization hits him that I will end him. He begins nodding frantically.

"Now that you understand you no longer have a daughter, let's make sure you remember that you never lay a hand on a woman or child again," I say, stepping back and taking a fighting stance.

When Bo releases him, he begins shaking his head no. It stops with my first punch, breaking his nose.

"Kick his ass, 'screech' Kick his ass!" the bird screeches again. The outcasts behind me are torn between laughing at the poor bird or watching me beat the shit out of Mia's Padre.

I throw a punch to his gut, and when he doubles over, I knee him in the face. He drops to the floor out cold. I look up at Bo, who is grinning at me, but now that my adrenaline is not pumping anymore, the pain in my ribs is killing me.

I grip my side tightly and wince. I'm immediately turned around, and Blaze has me in his hold. "You're injured," he says with concern, pulling me towards a hallway and pinning me to the wall.

"Let me see," he says, pushing my hand away. His eyes are so dark and intense as he looks down at me. Like he can see into my soul. The feel of his hand on mine sends tingles up my arm, and my nipples start to harden. Shit, what is he doing to me?

I sigh and raise my arms out of the way. Blaze lifts my shirt and sees the ace wraps I have on and the bruising around them. His eyes snap up to mine.

"Is this from the fight?" he asks, running his hands over the wraps.

"Yes, but I'll be fine," I reply, breathier than intended. Damn, this man's simple touch sets me on fire.

"You're done fighting Gia. I won't have you hurt," his deep baritone voice rumbles, leaving no room for argument.

It sends me into defense mode. "I don't react well to being ordered around Blaze," I say, leaning my face closer to his, which is difficult, seeing as I am 5 foot 8 inches, and he is about 6 foot 2 inches of pure muscle—a fine specimen of a man. Shit quit thinking like that, Gia, I chastise myself.

Blaze leans his face so close we are nearly touching. His warm, minty breath mingled with mine. He places both palms on the wall, caging me in, then pushes his thigh between my legs, separating mine.

Shit, it's pressing right up against my core, which is now wet.

"Gia," he growls, running his nose up the side of my face, and then he stops next to my ear while pressing his hard body into mine. My pulse is racing, and I grip the front of his cut.

"I admire how strong you are, Mi Alma," (my soulmate) he pauses, nibbling on my earlobe. My damn knees almost buckle at the feeling and his words.

"But I will destroy anyone who hurts you. So, no more fighting," he says, then kisses my cheek with those full, sexy lips I so desperately want on mine.

"You think you have the right to give me orders?" I question through ragged breaths.

He lowers his face again, so we are nose to nose. "You are mine now." he pauses, watching my reaction. My body is screaming hell yes, but my mind is trying to process his words.

"When you come to terms with that and are ready," he growls, running a hand from the top of my shoulder, over my collar bone, down between my breasts to the top of my jeans, and stops. His eyes snap back up, meeting mine.

My panties are soaked now, and I am aching to be touched.

"I will claim you in every way. Until then, I will try to give you time. Just promise me one thing, Mi Alma," (my soulmate) he says, placing his palm back on the wall.

"What's that?" I whisper.

"No man touches you but me," he studies my face, waiting for a reply, but I can't hold back the laugh that erupts out of me.

His eyebrows draw together, and he leans back, looking confused by my response. I push off the wall and stand against his large frame, tilting my chin.

"I've made it 21 years without letting a man get his hands on me. I'm sure I can handle a few more until one proves he is worthy of my heart," I say, meeting his stare head-on.

The look of shock at the revelation on his face is comical. But before my Nonna passed, she drilled into me that a man isn't worthy of your body if he hasn't won your heart. I have lived by that.

Blaze grabs me by the shoulders, pushing me back into the wall. I grip his cut as his lips come down onto mine.

They are warm and soft as they graze over my lips. Blaze slowly kisses me, then runs his tongue over my bottom lip. I open my mouth slightly to do the same to him, but his tongue pushes into my mouth.

His warm, minty taste hits my tastebuds as he buries his fingers in my hair and takes control of my movements. Tilting my head to the side, his tongue delves deep, massaging and caressing mine while we taste each other's mouths.

I try to rub my thighs together to get some relief, but he presses his huge leg in between mine, putting pressure on my core again. It's like he knows just what I need.

"I hate to interrupt you, love birds, but there's a bird out here going crazy, and we need to go," Bo's words make us break apart. We are both out of breath, and the look in Blaze's eyes tells me we will discuss this later.

I turn to Bo and smile. "Let's talk with a bird then," I say, walking past him. I know my cheeks must be red. He is going to tease me about this later.

When I enter the living room, a few of the Outcasts are tormenting the bird, and it's cursing them. "Leave it alone," I say, pushing my way through.

What I see almost makes me gag. The entire bottom of the cage is caked in shit, and the urine smell is rank. On top of that, the cage is too small for the bird. It can barely move a few steps in each direction.

"What's your name?" I ask.

It starts bobbing its head and whistles. "I'm the man," he says.

"Well, the man. Do you like living here in this shit whole?" I ask him.

"No, time to go. Time to go," he chirps.

I look around because I am not taking that filthy little cage. I spot a box with magazines in it sitting in the corner. I walk over, dump everything out, and walk back.

"I'll take you home with me, but first, we need to take a ride. Are you good with that?" I ask him, hearing laughter behind me, but I try to ignore it.

"Ride home, Ride home," the man says.

"Yes, now, for us to ride home, I need you in this box. Think you can handle that?" I ask.

He starts screeching and bobbing his head. I don't know what that means, but I won't leave him here with an abusive asshole. So, with determination, I open the door and reach in.

The man starts flapping his wings and screeching louder. "I'm not going to hurt you, man. I'm just taking you home with me. No one will ever hurt you," I say, trying to soothe him.

I feel a warm hand on my lower back and look over my shoulder, seeing Blaze smiling. I grin back, then refocus on the man. Taking a deep breath, I gently wrap my hand around him and pick him up.

His screeching stops, and he rubs his head against my wrist. I bring him to my chest. "I told you I wouldn't hurt you. Now, into the box to keep you safe for the ride."

As soon as I set him in the box, the screeching started again. I fold the flaps over it and hold it closed.

How the hell am I going to keep him in there and ride my bike without wrecking?

I look up into Blaze's face questioningly. He grins at me like he knows my dilemma.

"I'll strap it securely to the back of mine. I have a harness in the saddle bag I use for groceries," he says.

"Thank you," I hand him the man with a grin. We walk outside, leaving this awful house and Mia's Padre behind.

When I approach my bike, Bo throws his arm over my shoulder and grins at me. "So, Blaze, huh?" his eyes are twinkling with mischief.

"You have to admit he's hot as hell," I replied, flicking my gaze towards Blaze, who was finishing strapping the box into place but was watching Bo and me.

Bo follows my gaze and smiles. "He is a fine-looking man but too straight for my tastes."

I burst out laughing, making my ribs hurt, so I grabbed them, putting pressure.

Blaze's eyes are locked onto me and my hand that's holding my ribs. He's next to us in a few steps. "What are you two laughing about so hard that it has my woman in pain?" He asks with a rumble.

"Your woman, huh?" Bo asks, but you can hear the playfulness in it.

"Ya, didn't she tell you the news?" Blaze looks down as he pulls me away from Bo and takes me into his arms. He kisses the top of my head and then looks back at Bo.

"She was too busy talking about how hot you were," Bo retorts. I reach out to pinch his arm, but he jerks back out of reach, laughing.

"Come on, guys, I need to see how Mia is doing," I say, climbing onto my bike.

"I'm sure Cowboy is taking excellent care of her," Blaze chuckles.

His words confuse me as I think back to all the growling he was doing at the gym.

Everyone gets on their bikes, and we ride back to my apartment.

Chapter 6

Blaze

Gia is cruising alongside me as we enter Wells City. Everything about her feels right, like something deep inside me has clicked into place.

I grip the handlebars tighter as images of my past flash in my mind.

I glance over at her. Can she handle the darkness that's inside me? No, I never want that part of me to touch her. A part of me knows she is too good for me, but I can't let her go. I've never felt this way about a woman.

When we return to Pops gym, I park beside the stairs for Gia's apartment. She pulls beside me, followed by Bo and my fellow Outcast brothers.

I cut the engine off and immediately heard the bird screeching. What did he say his name was? The man, I chuckle and dismount to get the box unstrapped. It's early morning but still dark, so it takes me a minute.

When I finally get it released, Gia stands beside me, smiling. Damn, that sexy smile has my dick twitching.

She takes the box from me, and I place my hand on her back as we walk towards the stairs.

"Hey, Gia," Bo calls out, getting our attention, and I turn with her facing him.

"Want me to make a run to that 24-hour store to get food and supplies for the man?" He asks.

Fuck I didn't even think of that. I look at Gia; she looks from the box and then back at Bo. "Yes, do you know what I'll need? Because I have no idea," she says with a confused expression.

Bo laughs at her and nods. "He'll need pellets, a cage, perches, toys, food, water dishes, and a litter box," he rattles off like it's nothing. What the hell is he an expert on birds?

Gia tilts her head to the side. "Do I want to ask how you know that?" she says, and I chuckle.

"I watch videos at night to learn shit," he shrugs like it's nothing.

We all start laughing.

"Sure, get him whatever you think he needs," she says, then steps towards him with a curious expression." Why did you say litter box?"

"Because they can be litter trained if you put a perch over the box. Just reward them for using it with pistachios and shit. The video I watched said it could be done in 15 minutes," Bo replies with pride that he knows that.

"Well then, genius, that will be your job," Gia says with raised eyebrows and a grin. Bo walked right into that job, I think to myself.

She turns, giving me that megawatt smile, and I can't help myself. I lean down and kiss her before we climb the stairs.

As I step inside Gia's apartment for the first time, I scan the small space, taking in every detail: a small couch, coffee table, and TV.

To the side, I see a tiny kitchen with a bar and a dining room area off of it. What grabs my attention is the walls in the dining room. They are covered with old maps, drawings, and papers of scribbled notes. I look down at the small dining table with legal pads and papers strewn over it.

My feet carry me closer without conscious thought to get a better look. There are building schematics, copies of deeds, tax records, court records, and law books.

I look back at the wall covered in maps, realizing they are all of Freedom. What the hell is she up to? My eyes return to the legal pads on the table as conversation picks up across the room, but I ignore it.

I run my hand across the notes. No, it's a ledger of Jose and Raphel's routines and schedules. How long has she been watching them? It's a lot longer than I have by the dates next to the notations.

The legal pad I was reading is grabbed from the table and flipped over so I can't see it, and my head jerks up seeing Gia staring at me.

"What are you planning?" I can't stand the thought of her in danger. My brothers and I have been plotting to take out Jose and Raphel for a month. It all goes down next weekend. But this, I look around at everything Gia has been doing. It's like she's planning for war or a major corporate takeover.

"Blaze," Gia says, getting my attention and placing her hand on the center of my chest. "I've had one hell of a day and night. I'm running on no sleep, my ribs are aching, and I need to get Mia something to eat. She's hungry. Can we please talk about all of this later?"

I look at her, really look. Her face shows exhaustion: she's holding her side, but her eyes are asking me to let this go.

I step closer, stroke her cheek with my knuckles, and inhale her sweet cocoa butter scent. Leaning my face close to hers, I drop my voice low and deep. "We aren't done discussing this, Gia. I meant every word I said earlier. You're mine now, and your safety will always come first. All of this," I glance around and then meet her eyes. "We will talk when I return later," my words are final. She will tell me everything. One thing you learn fast in the military is that intel is crucial to any operation.

Her eyes study me with a hopeful look." Give me at least 7 hours to shower and get some sleep, then I will sit down and tell you everything. But Blaze," she pauses like she is choosing her words. I don't like that. She can always say anything to me.

"Don't let me down. I'm not one to give second chances." Her voice doesn't waiver, and her shoulders are stiff. She has been hurt or betrayed before.

I take her face in my hands, stroking my thumb over her bottom lip that I want to bite.

"I can't say that I will never screw up Gia. The best of people do. But I will never do anything to hurt or betray your trust. I am yours just as you are mine. You will realize that in time," I say, meaning every word.

"Whipped, 'cough,' 'cough,'" I hear Kane's taunting from across the room.

"Whipped," the man repeats Kane's taunt.

I don't move my eyes from Gia's, though. Fuck them all, they're just jealous.

"I'll be back in 7 hours, Mi Alma," (my soulmate) I say, my voice low and gravelly, threading my fingers into her silky hair.

She nods slightly, and I lean down, barely grazing my lips over hers in a soft, chased kiss. As I reluctantly pull away, my heart is pounding, and my cock's screaming for me to claim her, making her mine. I force myself to take a step back. If she needs time, I'll give her that.

Gia raises her hand and traces her lips. I turn towards the door because if I don't leave now, I never will.

"Let's load up," I announce, looking around at my brothers as I walk to the door. They all head my way, but I notice Cowboy isn't here.

I look at Kane with a questioning look. "You and Cowboy stayed behind to take care of Mia. Where the fuck is he?"

Kane chuckles and shakes his head.

"Man, he's in the bedroom with her. Won't leave her side even while she sleeps," he says, pointing to a door off the living room.

I grin and nod. I guess I'm not the only one whipped by a woman this week. Grabbing the doorknob, I glance over my shoulder at Gia one last time before I walk out. She is watching us, her fingertips still touching her lips. I wink and walk out. Just for now, though. I'm not usually a patient man; 7 hours of going without her will be hell.

We reach the parking lot and straddle our bikes as three black SUVs pull in, parking across from us. I put the key in the ignition but paused, watching closely. If trouble is coming to Pops or Gia, my brothers and I will handle it.

I cross my arms over my chest and lean back on the seat. My brothers all sit straighter, ready to deal with shit like we were trained to.

Men in suits get out of 2 SUVs first. My eyes flick down to their waists, and they're armed. I uncross my arms and slide a hand under the back of my cut, touching my Glock.

A broad man, probably Italian in descent, gets out of the driver's seat of the middle SUV and opens the back door. A man in his 60's exits, buttoning his suit jacket. He is large and muscular for his age and exudes power and authority. He's definitely in charge. Where have I seen him before?

Then it hits me. That's Mr. D'Angelo, the former Don before he handed things over to his son. He eyes us with interest, then reaches into the SUV, retrieving two bakery boxes.

He confidently strides in our direction, stopping a few feet in front of my bike.

"Mr. Cruz, I'm surprised to see you here. People say you rarely travel to Wells City even to see your Papa," his voice shows no emotion matching his expression. Indicating he is a man used to keeping things close to the vest.

I lean forward, placing my forearm on the handlebars. "Your informants are correct. However, it's always good to change things up sometimes to keep people on their toes," I retort with a raised brow.

I fear no man. Spending too many years on missions, I've faced down more than a few enemies and walked away from every one of them alive. They can't say the same.

Mr. D'Angelo belts out a deep, hearty chuckle at my response. "It's always good to keep people guessing. Expect the unexpected, I always say." He turns, walking up the stairs to Gia's with his men close behind.

So much for her getting the sleep she wanted, I think as I start the engine to return to the bar. I could use a few hours of shut eye myself. Seven hours, I chant as my brothers, and I roar out of the parking lot towards Freedom.

Chapter 7

Gia

The exhaustion from yesterday and last night finally weighs on me as I drag myself into the kitchen and put a pot of coffee on. I need to make Mia and Cowboy something to eat. He may have eaten recently, but who knows when Mia has.

Once the coffee is perking, I turn towards the fridge and pull ingredients out for omelets. I'll need to make four if I include Bo and myself.

As I plate the last one, there is a knock at the door. Thinking it's Bo, but he must have his hands full, I yell, "Be right there." To my surprise, Nonno enters, followed by his men.

I smile wide and drop everything, walking to him. He chuckles as I hug his waist. "I didn't expect you this early," I say, smiling at him.

"I thought it would be nice to have breakfast with my Piccola," (little one) Nonno says, grinning at me.

"I'm not so little anymore," I poke him in the ribs, making him chuckle. "Do you want an omelet?" I ask, returning to the stove, ready to cook for him.

"I brought your favorite pastries," he replies, sitting two boxes on the bar, and my stomach chooses that moment to growl.

"Ok, I'll eat pastries. You sit and eat an omelet. I know you prefer a hot breakfast anyway," I reply, setting silverware next to a plate for him. He smiles and then looks towards the dining room, no doubt wondering why we are eating at the bar and not at a real table like he is used to at home.

His eyes go wide when he takes in the mess. Maps are on the walls, and books and papers are all over the table. He looks back at me with a raised brow as he sits on the stool, waiting for me to explain.

"Can we eat and visit before the heavy conversation starts?" I ask. My Papa, no, he isn't that anymore; Anthony D'Angelo never deserved my respect or love. But my Nonno has always had both. I'm relieved when he nods his agreement, and I pour us all coffee, including his men. They retrieve their cups without a word, walking away.

I sit beside Nonno and begin devouring an apple fritter like it's my last meal, making him laugh.

"You always loved anything with apples, even as a child," he says as if recalling my childhood memories.

My heart clenches, remembering how my Nonna would bake things with apples in them just for me. Or we would sit in the kitchen at night before bed when I stayed with them. She would peel an apple while we talked, taking turns eating slices like it was our girl time together.

"I did," I say, studying his face. His eyes show a hint of sadness in them. "I miss her too," I whisper.

He reaches over, patting my hand, and we continue to eat silently for a few minutes. However, in true Don D'Angelo style, he changes the subject and is very direct.

"Tell me about Mr. Cruz and his men being outside when I arrived. The gym is closed at this time of day, so he wasn't here to see his Padre," his tone is no-nonsense, and his eyes say protective mode.

I wipe my hands on a napkin and drink my coffee just as Cowboy enters the kitchen. "Mia's hungry," he growls like he is ready to go on a rampage if someone doesn't feed her.

I raise a challenging eyebrow at him using that tone, and he turns away. "Breakfast is on the counter, coffee is in the pot. Are you taking it to her, or am I?" I realized what a stupid question that was after I asked it. He has been hovering over her like a love-sick puppy since he first laid eyes on her.

Cowboy doesn't answer, just grumbles under his breath, grabbing a serving tray in the corner. He places two plates with omelets and two cups of coffee and walks out. I guess that's my answer.

I look back at Nonno, who is staring at me, waiting for me to explain what the hell is going on. In case he missed part, I take a deep breath and recap everything from yesterday at the worst birthday dinner ever. Then, I go through the rest of my night.

I do leave out the hot kissing and touching part with Blaze because no Nonno wants to hear that. However, I include the part about Blaze claiming me as his when I'm ready.

"You haven't slept?" Nonno asked, but it's more of a statement. I shake my head in response.

"You're claiming this young woman Mia as family?" he asks.

"Si," I reply firmly. She has been like a younger sister to me for years. Now, she will be in all ways that matter.

Nonno nods. "I want to meet her once she recovers," he says, and I grin. Mia doesn't know it yet, but she's getting a new Nonno.

"This young man, Angel, do you feel the same for him?" Nonno asks, and I look at him confused, making him chuckle.

"I may not be Don anymore, but I make it a point to know who my only grandchild is around. When you moved above Cruz's gym, I looked into the family. The owner, who goes by Big C, settled in Freedom. Latino background with good family values by all accounts. His wife passed, leaving him to raise his only son, Angel," Nonno states as if it's nothing.

My shock must be written all over my face that he knows more about Blaze than I do at this point because there is a twinkle in his eyes.

"Do you want me to go on?" he asks. I nod and pick up my coffee, anxious to learn everything I can about Blaze.

"By all accounts, this Angel, or Blaze as they call him now, is a good man. He enlisted in the Navy just after his 18th birthday, worked hard, and was accepted into the Seal program. After going through BUD/S, Angel spent years rising through the ranks to Command Master Chief. Rumor has it that the last mission he led his unit on went south. There was nothing more I could find out about it as records are sealed or heavily redacted, but every unit member still alive was discharged after that. They all settled in Freedom or Wells City, forming the Outcast MC not long ago," Nonno takes the last bite of his omelet as I digest everything, he has told me.

I have never been drawn or attracted to a man, but Blaze sets every part of me on fire when he's around. I can't imagine what he or his brothers went through. But one thing I know for sure is that he pushes Big C away. Why though? Is it because of what happened on that mission? Will he hold back on me or push me away if I get too close? He says he wants me to be his, but does he know what that will mean? I'll never settle for less than the loving relationship Nonno and Nonna had.

"What's going through that head, Piccola?" Nonno's question brings me out of my thoughts.

"Blaze pushes his Papa away, and according to Big C, they were so close before he enlisted," I shake my head, gathering my thoughts.

"I will never settle for half a partner or just part of any man. I want what you and Nonna had or nothing at all," I say, meeting his eyes. My chest aches at the thought of walking away from what could be with Blaze. But I won't live in an unhappy relationship. I've seen too many people do it.

Nonno's face softens at my words, and he takes my hand. "Never settle for anything, Piccola. You are a D'Angelo demand the best." His words are firm, and his eyes look towards the dining room.

He pulls me to a standing position with him. "Come and tell me what you are up to. Retirement is boring for an old man."

I burst out laughing, making him smile at me. I point at him accusingly. "First, Nonno, you may be officially retired, but nothing happens in Wells City you don't know about. Secondly, 61 is not old. In your prime is what I'd call you," I say, looking him over.

My Nonno maybe 61, but with our Italian heritage, he doesn't look much older than 50. He is 6 foot 3 inches and built like a tank due to his daily workouts. Add in the power and authority he commands from his days of being Don D'Angelo; nobody messes with my Nonno.

He throws his head back and belts out a deep belly laugh at my words. When he finishes, his face goes dead serious. "Start talking."

I nod because I trust Nonno more than anyone. Well, except for Bo. Nonno's opinion and experience can help.

Squeezing his hand, I lead him to the wall and go over the maps of Freedom, the recent corruption that led to the Mayor of Wells City, and the routines I have been following.

Then, I showed him the laws I had researched and my short-term and long-term plans. When I have given all the cliff notes, he slides his hands into his pockets, and his face goes blank.

I know that look. It is no doubt a practiced expression when he is in deep thought. He stands in front of the maps, studying them closely, then steps over to the schematics I have of a water tower and a new warehouse. He points to the warehouse. "What is the new build for?"

"If I am taking over an entire town and rebuilding, it will be by my rules, meaning new laws. That is for legal fighting and gambling in Freedom," I say, determined.

His lip twitches, but he doesn't say a thing and looks back at the maps. "Why is the old Grand Hotel circled in red?" he asks but leans closer, reading the notes I scribbled below it on the map. His head jerks towards me, and I giggle.

"Once I take out Jose and Raphel, the Grand Hotel will be renovated as my home," I pause, seeing the surprise on his face. Nothing usually surprises him.

"As for the notes below it, I had planned on keeping that a secret." I grin, then continue. "During renovations, I will have the entrance to the basement hidden because I want a fully functioning Crematorium built.

Nonno's expression shouldn't surprise me when it shows admiration for my forethought. Hell, he's probably wondering why he never thought of building one.

"I may have to put that part of the plan on hold, though," I tell him. I'm sure he can hear the disappointment in my voice.

"Over the years, I have put some money back, well over 50 thousand from fighting. But that's not enough to renovate a town and buy the arsenal and men Bo and I will need to protect it," I admit.

Nonno's face turns from blank into an I know something you don't look, and he smirks at me. What is he thinking? When I disowned my parents and told Anthony he could shove my trust fund up his ass, that was it. At that moment, my plans for the future altered.

"You're thinking of the trust you no longer have," he says with a knowing look, and I nod.

"Well, Piccola, my son has always been a disappointment. I don't know where your Nonna or I went wrong with him. He has always been more like my disgrace of a brother than me," Nonno says, shaking his head and sighing.

"Anyway, I would have never let him force you into marriage. As for your trust, Nonna and I made one for you when you were 10. Now that you are old enough," he turns, smiling at the maps.

"And obviously, know what you want from life; I will release it. Meet me at Wells City Bank at 3 pm, and we will get the paperwork finalized."

My mouth feels dry, and my heart is pounding in my chest. Did he just say what I think he said? I mean, I have always known Nonno had my back and loved me. But to set up a trust to ensure a future is beyond anything I could have imagined. I always planned on working hard and building things myself, knowing how my awful family was. I feel tears building, and one escapes, running down my cheek.

"You didn't have to do that, Nonno," I whisper, barely able to speak.

He raises his large hand, wiping the tear from my cheek and cupping my face. "You are loved Gianna. Maybe not by everyone who should have loved you, but you, my Piccola, have always been so very loved."

His face goes from caring to stern, and he drops his hand. "As a D'Angelo, you never show weakness to outsiders. Family is fine, but never anyone else." I wipe my face and straighten my shoulders because he is right. I have seen capos fall with the first sign of weakness. That won't happen to me.

He turns, looking at the maps again. "You said the corruption leads back to our Mayor?" he asks.

"Si Nonno. Bo and I have been tracking both Jose and Raphel. They give him kickbacks for leaving them alone and looking the other way. The city owns Freedom even though it's 25 miles away," I say, pointing to the papers on the table.

"They have even been distributing into Wells City quietly and bussing in the hookers from the Grand Hotel to the club at the edge of town to work out of on Wednesday nights," I tell him, and his head jerks in my direction.

"I hadn't been informed of this. Why would my son allow this?" he half asks. Then what I have suspected all along hits him. The kickbacks don't stop at the Mayor. Don Anthony D'Angelo is getting them, too. Otherwise, they couldn't operate in Wells City.

This means that my former dear old Papa has been allowing drugs into schools and is allowing men to operate here who used to snatch young girls off the street to put them to work.

I watch realization take over Nonno's face, which contorts to anger. I have rarely seen him angry. He is always composed and calculated.

"You will have plenty of money to do this and be comfortable for the rest of your life. But Piccola, you must know you and Bo cannot do this alone," he says with a firm tone.

I knew that after we took out Jose and Raphel, we would need men to remove their crew and clear the town for me to take over. "I'll hire the help I need."

Nonno shakes his head. "Loyalty can't be bought Piccola; it is freely given. Most importantly is keeping it, and that only happens out of respect. They must respect your authority and your command." He says, pointing to the center map with the Grand Hotel circled in red.

"To be not just a leader but a D'Angelo leading comes with great responsibility if you are to run your own family. It will be much the same as when I run Wells City. Make every decision, weigh the outcomes carefully, and be ready to live with the consequences of every action and choice you make. Most importantly, choose your family members wisely," he says, stepping closer, and I absorb every word he says.

"You always have me in your corner, and I will have another gift for you when we meet this afternoon," he says, and I raise my arms, wrapping them around his waist.

"You have done so much already. All I need is you and your love, Nonno," I say, squeezing him tight.

"Oh, my Piccola. You will always have me, but you will like this gift. Call it a lesson in how you take what you want using leverage," he says, then chuckles.

I look up at him and grin. Nonno is the epitome of what every man should be. He was an amazing husband and father, no matter how Anthony turned out. An incredible Don and the best Nonno anyone could ask for. They need to duplicate him, I think, then laugh.

He raises an eyebrow, but I just shake my head. "Get some sleep, and I'll see you at the bank at 3 pm," he says firmly, stepping away.

I smile, "Si Nonno. Ti amo." (I love you)

"Ti amo Piccola," he says, turning and striding out the door, his men following.

I look around at the dishes and sigh just as Bo enters the apartment arms loaded with a cage and numerous bags, looking proud of himself. I laugh and shake my head. For a big, tough guy, his personality is always the joker at home.

The man comes swooping into the kitchen, landing on the bar, chirping happily at not being in a cage. I pick up the spatula and point it at him. "If you go potty in the kitchen, it's time out for you," I state firmly.

"Time out, no time out," he says, rocking back and forth, and Bo laughs at us.

"Don't worry, I'll have his things set up in a few minutes," Bo says, unpacking everything.

"I made breakfast if you're hungry," I tell him, and he nods in thanks.

With an exhausted sigh, I walk towards my bedroom, looking inside. Mia is asleep again, and Cowboy sits on the bed with his back against the headboard. His arms crossed over his chest, and his eyes closed.

The door creaks slightly, and his eyes open, looking at me. "I was checking on her," I say quietly. He nods at me, and I step inside, taking a tank top, shorts, and panties out of my dresser and then sneaking back out.

A quick shower for me, then a nap on the couch will have to do since I have to meet Nonno later. Then it hits me. Damn, Blaze will be here later, also.

I lay my things on the counter in the bathroom and realized something. The pain in my ribs is getting better quickly. I guess Iron Maiden didn't fracture any. They're just bruised.

Chapter 8

Gia

I slowly open my eyes, feeling a vibration on my arm. Once my eyes focus, I realize I'm on the couch, and the man is sleeping on me. His head is tucked down into his feathers, and his body vibrates occasionally.

"At least he likes someone," I hear Mia's voice, followed by a deep chuckle.

I look towards the kitchen seeing Mia and Bo sitting at the bar eating sandwiches.

"Does he not like people?" I ask her. She should know his behavior, having lived in the same house as him.

She shakes her head no as she swallows the bite she was chewing. "The only person he has ever liked was Madre," her face shows sadness at the memory.

"Why is he on me then?" I ask just as the man raises his head.

Mia laughs and then winces, no doubt because her lip hasn't healed yet. She looks at Bo. "Genius here was working on litter training him and told him he had to listen, or mama bear would put him in time out," she says laughing.

"Then the man kept saying mama bear, so Bo went with it," she shrugs, taking another bite of her sandwich.

"Ya, I went to the couch, pointed, and told him you were momma bear and to be a good boy," Bo said with a chuckle.

"After giving him a few pistachios, he flew over to you and went to sleep," Bo says with a cocky smirk.

I slowly raise my hand and stroke the man's head. "I'll be your momma if you'll be a good boy and use the litter box," I tell him.

He dips his head down, enjoying my touch. "Good boy, Good boy," he says.

"What time is it?" I say quickly, wondering how long I slept.

"Just after 2 pm, why?" Bo asks with raised brows.

"I have to meet Nonno at the Bank at 3 pm." I answer, sitting up and pissing off the man, making him squawk at me.

Bo turns so he is fully facing me. "What's up?"

I grin at him. "It seems Nonno has secretly had my back more than I thought. I do have a trust fund, just not from where I assumed."

The shock on Bo's face, I'm sure, looked a lot like mine did when Nonno told me about it.

"Do you want me to stay here this time?" Bo asks. Damn, he not only always has my back but is so considerate.

"No, Bo. We have never had secrets, and we won't start now. This plan," I point towards the dining room, glancing at the maps and research we did together.

"Our plan is just that. Ours. We build a town and a better life together. Not just for us, but for everyone like us," I say firmly.

Mia turns, looking towards the dining room. Her eyes take in our mess, and then she looks from Bo to me. "What's going on?" she asks.

"Bo can explain while I get ready to meet Nonno. By the way, where is Cowboy?" I ask, getting up.

"He's sleeping," Mia sighs, then looks at her sandwich.

"He's got the hots for you," I say with a grin, walking into the bathroom to get ready.

Once I've used the bathroom and brushed my hair and teeth, I find Bo standing by the door waiting for me. I look over to Mia, who's standing in front of the maps, taking notes on a legal pad. "Are you staying here?" I ask her.

She turns with a smile. "Ya, and I want to help," she says, pointing her pencil at the table.

"Good, all of the organizational skills you used at the center are about to be put to good use," I say with a smile.

"What do you mean?" she asks, scrunching her eyebrows together.

"How does the title town planner sound?" I ask.

Her face lights up, and her eyes sparkle. "It sounds good to me. What exactly will be my duties?"

"Overseeing town projects like new builds and renovations. Anything for the growth and betterment of the town," I reply.

Her smile is back, and she looks around at everything. "I'll get started while you're gone," she chirps happily.

"The Grand Hotel will need to be at the top of the list. It will be our home," I say, and she nods firmly.

Bo chuckles beside me and opens the door for us.

Once we arrive at the bank and park, I see Nonno's SUV and his men talking and smoking beside it. Bo and I walk in their direction, but Sammy, his main bodyguard, points toward the building, and I nod, changing directions.

"I'll wait here," Bo says once we reach the lobby, and he sits in a chair.

A lady in a suit approaches me while I look around for any sign of Nonno. "Miss D'Angelo, they're waiting for you upstairs," she says politely, gesturing for me to follow her.

We enter an elevator and go to the 7th floor. Once we exit, she goes to the right, knocking twice on a large wooden door. The nameplate reads President A. Stone.

"Enter," comes a deep voice. She opens the door but steps aside for me to go in. Once I enter, she shuts the door, leaving.

Nonno is sitting in an armchair in a seating area by floor-to-ceiling windows. An older bald gentleman in a suit is seated on the other side of a coffee table. He immediately stands with a broad smile, hand outstretched to shake mine.

I take it and chuckle dryly. People seem very friendly when you have the D'Angelo name or see you are about to come into money. I dislike him already.

My eyes go to Nonno, and the look he gives me says my laugh doesn't fool him and knows what I'm thinking. I take a seat in the chair close to Nonno.

For the next 30 minutes, I listen dumbfounded as Mr. Stone goes over the trust being released, and I numbly decide to put half in a checking and half in a savings account. At the same time, I decline his suggestions for CDs and other investments. I don't understand what that shit is entirely, so it's not for me.

I know I will need easy access to a lot of money for my plans, just not the exact amount. So, for now, this is what I will do with it. The number keeps ringing in my head while he and Nonno talk like old business acquaintances. Sixty million dollars. Sixty fucking million, I keep repeating in my head, and I sign paper after paper. I have always known my family were billionaires, but it never affected me.

The rebellious one who refused to take orders never got the perks that a good princess would. No, I never even had a car given to me. I've always worked for anything I had unless it came from Nonno or Nonna.

As I sign the last paper and slide it across the coffee table, Nonno asks Mr. Stone to leave us for a few minutes so we can talk.

He gets up and walks out of his office like it's nothing, making me giggle. Turning towards Nonno, I grin. "Everyone does as you say, don't they?"

He smirks and raises a brow, then his expression goes serious as he pulls two files from a briefcase, handing them to me.

"These are the presents I told you about," he says, and I take them but don't open them. I study his face, waiting for him to speak.

"When you buy something like you were planning to buy Freedom from Wells City, it makes it yours. However, what happens when you make it all nice and shiny? A place worth having?" He asks me.

I'm confused for a moment until he speaks again.

"First, in buying it, there is no statement. It's just a purchase. Take it, and it's yours just the same, but you have sent a message," he says, and I nod, understanding now. Send a loud enough message, and people won't mess with me in the future.

"Secondly, once you make Freedom profitable and a decent place to live, increasing its value, others will want it. Be sure to take these two out of that equation first. In those files is enough information to accomplish both simultaneously," he says, pointing to the files in my hand.

I look down and open the top one. I flip through it, scanning everything. There are photographs of the mayor's sexual activities that I could have gone the rest of my life without seeing.

Records of bank accounts in the U.S. and overseas, phone records with highlighted phone numbers I recognize of Anthony, Jose, and Raphel, and a number I don't recognize. A police report is at the back of the file, paperclipped to court transcripts. It seems he and a judge conspired to get his son out of a vehicular manslaughter charge where the son was accused of a DUI. The charges were dismissed.

I jerk my head up to Nonno, and he nods toward the other file.

When I open it, I see the same last name as the Mayor of Wells City with a photo of a man in a Sheriff's Uniform. I read the paperwork behind it, and he is just as corrupt. He is the Sheriff in the next county and does dirty work when needed for our Mayor.

I close both files and lean back, staring out the window. With these, I can force the Mayor to hand over Freedom, which was only used for him to gain illegal money anyway. There is enough information in both files to make sure that neither he nor his Sheriff cousin ever bothers us.

I run my hand over the files as warmth spreads through me. There have only ever been four people who have cared for me, and one of them is gone—my Nonna.

I look at the incredible man beside me with so much adoration and love.

"You have no idea what you mean to me, Nonno. And not because of this," I say, gesturing towards the files and the door where the bank president left earlier.

"Just knowing that I have you means more than what I have words to express." I feel tears welling up in my eyes, and he stiffens.

Shit, he hates public displays of feelings, but I can't help it. Nonno leans forward, taking my chin between his fingers, and holds my gaze.

"I should have taken you years ago and raised you as my own. Consider this my apology, and in the future," his eyes search mine for a moment before he continues, and my heart is pounding in my chest, waiting to hear the words.

"From now on, you are Piccola Ragazza," (baby girl) he says, and I feel like my heart will beat out of my chest.

I nod and choke back the tears as I whisper, "Ti amo Nonno." Hearing him say that I am his baby girl is overwhelming.

"Ti amo," he replies, drying my eyes with his fingertips. "Now, one more thing," Nonno says, sitting straighter. "10 of my men will accompany you tonight. You said you wanted to hit them at 4 am?" he asks.

I square my shoulders, sitting straighter also. "Si, they will be unsuspecting then," I reply.

"They will meet you at your apartment at 3 am prepared," his tone is low and his words final.

"Si," I reply, grateful for his help.

"Oh, and Gia," he says, eyeing me. "I will arrange for my personal contractor to meet you at the old Grand Hotel at 8 am. Just tell him everything you need. He is discreet."

I grin as his words sink in. This contractor can do everything I need, including the secret entrance to the basement I want and the crematorium.

The office door opens, getting our attention, and we stand. Mr. Stone enters with a questioning look.

"We are finished here," my Nonno says.

As I clutch the files to my chest walking towards the door, I pause in front of Mr. Stone. "I'm going to need one more thing before I go," I say matter of fact.

"Anything, Miss D'Angelo," he replies, and I cringe. I've always hated people who are kiss asses.

"Cash and something to carry it in," I say firmly.

"How much would you like to withdraw today?" he says with a more serious tone.

"A million would be nice," I reply with a smirk. Nonno chuckles, squeezing my shoulder, then walks out, shaking his head.

I look back at Mr. Stone with a raised brow, waiting for him to start downstairs with me so we can make a withdrawal. "Miss D'Angelo, we don't keep that kind of money on the premises. No bank does, for that matter. I can double-check and see what I can do, though," he says with a hopeful look, but his hands are fidgeting.

Does he think I will shoot him for not giving me what I want? "Please do," I say politely.

He walks to his phone and makes a call. A few minutes later, after talking numbers with someone, he says two tellers will be up with $500 thousand in 30 minutes if that is acceptable. I nod and smile, sitting in front of his desk while he talks to them, giving instructions.

"Tell them to send the tall blonde biker sitting in the lobby up too, please," I say with a smile, interrupting him.

He nods and relays my message. It's only a few minutes before the lady from earlier escorts Bo into the office.

He smiles at me, but his eyes hold questions. I grin as he sits but slightly shake my head so he knows we will talk later.

Bo nods and kicks back, stretching his legs out like he is at home. We only have to wait 20 minutes before a man and woman enter carrying a weird-looking duffle bag with the bank's logo.

I stand with a smile, and Bo steps to my side. "Do I want to know what's in that?" He asks.

I look at him and grin. "I'm sure many people would like to know what's in it."

He shakes his head and chuckles.

After I signed all the necessary paperwork for my withdrawal, Bo and I strolled out of the bank to our bikes.

"All right, Gia, what's going on?" Bo asks, standing between me and my bike with his arms crossed. His body language says he isn't moving until I talk.

"Look, I'm not just standing here in the middle of the damn city with this," I say, holding the bag of money in my hand higher, gesturing to it, "while we have a heart-to-heart. Let's do a little shopping, and I'll explain everything at the apartment," I state as I walk around him to my bike.

"OK, just answer one question so I know how alert I need to be. How much?" he points to the bag.

"They could only part with 500k today," I shrug.

Bo coughs through a laugh, then mounts his bike, starting the engine. When he looks back at me, his face is serious. "Where to first?"

"Guns and ammo," I say as I put the files in the bag and secure it behind me. Then, start my baby up.

Nodding at Bo, we pull out of the parking lot and head to the gun store before going home.

Chapter 9

Blaze

I place my palms on the shower wall and lean my head forward, letting the hot water rush over me. I didn't sleep worth a shit thinking about Gia and the pricks here in Freedom.

She may be a mafia princess, but the thought of her being in danger is twisting my gut into knots. Maybe if I order her to stay behind, she'll listen. I chuckle at the thought. I can guess why she's called 'Rebel,' but not because she follows orders.

My dick twitches as I recall how strong and capable, she was in the ring.

I quickly wash and get out of the shower. The need to see Gia and kiss those delicious lips again drives me to move faster.

When I'm dressed and exit the bedroom, I see Axel, Hawk, Kane, and Thor sitting around the living room. I don't miss a step as I head for the kitchen for a cup of coffee before we leave.

"Is Cowboy still with Mia?" Kane asks with a chuckle.

"He was when I left Gia this morning," I reply, then savor that first gulp of hot coffee someone had already perked.

"We heading over to compare her intel to ours and make a plan?" Hawk asks, standing and ready for some action as usual. I smirk, knowing how much he loves a good fight.

"Ya, we leave in 5. Hunter downstairs at the bar?" I ask, looking around. They all nod, knowing this will be hard on him. Since things went to shit on our last mission, he has been trapped in that damn wheelchair. There's nothing worse on a man like us than confining them. That wheelchair might as well be a prison sentence, but he refuses to let them operate again, removing the last of the shrapnel from his spine.

I shake my head to get rid of those thoughts. He has every right to choose his path in life, even if I disagree with his decision.

I swallow the last of my coffee and sit the cup down. "Let's head out and see what we can learn, if anything, from Gia and Bo," I say, grabbing my wallet, phone, and Glock.

We all walk out of the apartment and downstairs to the bar, our boots hitting the old wood steps like a stampede coming.

Once downstairs, I see Hunter behind the bar drying glasses. He looks up, eyeing us with longing in his eyes. I hate seeing that look on my fellow brother.

"You got things covered here until we get back?" I ask, hopefully making him feel useful.

Hunter gives me a firm nod and goes back to drying that damn glass, and my stomach twists. I have to ignore it. Pity is something I'll never let him see from me. The man is a hero, and I'll always treat him with the respect he deserves.

I scan the bar, seeing the prospects sitting around, and shake my head. Their asses will prove themselves later tonight or be kicked to the curb.

When I pull out onto the road with Axel, Hawk, Kane, and Thor behind me, the roar of our engines reverberates off the surrounding buildings.

I have one thing on my mind right now: seeing my woman. The added intel and learning their plan of attack is secondary.

We pull into the parking lot of Pop's gym, and I notice that Gia and Bo's bikes aren't there. My jaw clenches, wondering where she is and who she's with. Every protective instinct in me is screaming to find her.

I tap that shit down and park. My brothers do the same.

I glance over seeing Cowboy's bike. I dismount and take the stairs two at a time. He better know where she is and when she'll be back.

When I reach her door, I don't hesitate pounding on it impatiently. Cowboy swings the door open with his gun in hand and a fierce look.

I hear deep chuckles behind me, and I smirk.

"Where is she?" I ask as I push by him into her apartment. I scan the open space, seeing Mia at the dining table, working on a laptop and taking notes on a legal pad.

I swing my head back at Cowboy because he hasn't answered my question.

"Gia and Bo went to meet Nonno at the bank. They will be back soon," Mia says, answering for him.

I walk towards her, taking in her bruised face. "Are you feeling better?" I ask, and Cowboy steps beside me, a low growl rumbling from his chest.

I quirk an eyebrow at him because all my men know better than to disrespect me. Firstly, I led and trained them for years as their Command Master Chief. Secondly, I will beat their ass for disgracing the cut on his back and the oath he took to the club for behavior unbecoming of an officer in the Outcasts.

Cowboy nods, realizing his mistake, and sits at the table closest to Mia without a word.

"I'm fine," Mia says, not looking up from the laptop.

That is a practiced response, and we both know it. I stand firm, crossing my arms over my chest, staring at her until she raises her head.

Mia sighs, leaning back in her chair. "I'm ok, just sore. One of the best lessons I've learned in the past few years is that no matter how bad family knocks you down or what people say about you, none of it matters. It just makes you stronger. Move on and be you," she says with a stern look.

"Who taught you that philosophy?" I ask, but my gut already knows the answer.

"Gia," is all she says, confirming my suspicions. I shake my head, wondering what my woman's life has been like. Not what people whisper about behind her back or what I've heard. I need to find out.

I hear the rumble of motorcycles outside and go to the window. Gia and Bo are parking their bikes next to ours. Her gaze meets mine, and my heart starts pounding against my ribs at the sight of her.

Pops pulls in, and her attention shifts to his truck. He gets out and walks to her, pointing at the bags behind her I hadn't noticed before. Shit, Bo's bike is loaded down too. What have they been up to?

Gia stands and talks to Pop for a few minutes, then he hugs her, making warmth spread through me. Anyone else touching her, and I would be ready to hurt them. But seeing how my Pop's cares for her does something to me.

He treats her like a daughter; once I make her mine, she will be. I grin at the thought.

They unload the bikes and start up the stairs. When I turn, everyone is staring at me with cocky looks on their faces.

"You claiming her as your Ol' Lady?" Thor asks, and I give him the are you stupid look.

"As soon as she's ready, I'll bring it to church," I say firmly.

Several of my brothers pound their fists on their thighs, and a couple of whoops are heard, making me smile.

Gia enters the apartment with Bo right behind her. On instinct, my eyes drift lower. She is wearing a black tank that's stretched to accommodate her ample breasts, showing just enough cleavage to make me want to drop to my knees to worship her like the goddess she is.

Her faded jeans cling tightly to her perfect round ass and thick thighs I want to have wrapped around me.

Seeing that she has a bag in each hand, I look up, and our eyes lock. A sexy smile spreads on her beautiful face.

I am in front of her in 4 long strides, needing to get my hands on her. Raising my hand, I thread my fingers into her hair and grip the back of her neck as she looks up at me with those big brown eyes making my cock twitch.

"I don't like being away from you," I say, grumbling lowly.

Gia's smile widens, and her cheeks flush. "I have been thinking about you too," she says, tilting her face back more.

I take the hint and lean down, tasting those full, luscious lips I've been craving since this morning. A throat clearing makes her pull away, and I growl, looking up at Bo.

He is smiling like the cat who ate the canary at us.

"Mama's home," the man says excitedly, landing on the kitchen bar and bobbing his head from side to side.

I look at Mia, but she is looking at Gia, laughing. When Gia starts chuckling, I get it now. He's calling Gia Mama. I shake my head and take the bags from Gia to set them down, but she grips one tighter, making me look closer at it.

The side of the bag says Wells City Bank and my head snaps up, looking at her in question. "You're walking around with a bag full of cash?" I ask, knowing that in this city, that isn't smart. Then again, who is dumb enough to mess with a D'Angelo?

She giggles and nods. Bo walks away laughing. "She wanted a cool million, but they didn't have it in the safe," he sings songs like that's normal. Who the fuck walks into a bank asking for that kind of money?

I stare at Gia until she sighs. "I'll explain everything. Let me grab a cup of coffee and sit."

I put the bag I took from her on the floor next to the dining table and stand beside a vacant chair waiting.

Once she has a cup of coffee, she and Bo sit, and I follow suit next to her. She takes a drink and smiles, then looks at me intently, studying my face before she looks around the room at my brothers, who have now all crowded into the room.

She sets her cup down and stands again, walking to the maps and pointing at the largest of the three, Freedom.

"As you can tell, we have been monitoring Freedom, as well as Jose and Raphel, for almost two years. Everything has been logged carefully, from their business dealings in drugs and prostitution to their personal lives. Including who is covering for them and getting kickbacks." Gia pauses, looking around at each of us before continuing.

"Today, additional information on them fell into my hands that will help with our long-term plan, but for now, I only want to discuss the short term," she says, eyeing us, but Bo leans forward like he is dying to say something, but she shakes her head at him to wait.

"Tonight, or 4 am, we will strike, taking out both of them and clearing the town afterward. Twenty original D'Angelo men will be here at 3 am armed and ready to follow orders. If you are going to get involved, we can split into two groups, taking them out simultaneously instead of one at a time," Gia says, looking at me.

"Oh, we are more than involved, Gia," I state firmly, crossing my arms. I need to explain to her what it means to be mine.

She smiles and nods. "Jose and Raphel shut everything down by 3 am according to their past schedule, so 4 am is perfect for catching them off guard or in bed. If we split into two groups, Hitting the Grand Hotel," she says, pointing to the other map with the old hotel circled in red.

"Simultaneously hitting the apartment complex, taking them all out, they can't warn each other—we clean house. Any armed man or woman is to be put down; the prostitutes will be escorted out of town and warned never to return. I want Freedom cleared of all corruption, drugs, and prostitution before the sun rises tomorrow." Gia leans against the wall, folding her arms over her chest with a grin. Fuck she is hot as hell when she takes charge. But that's not how this is going to go.

I stand, and with long strides, I am now towering over her. "Mind if I take a look?" I ask, but it's not a question. She nods, but that little pink tongue comes out, licking her bottom lip.

I have to force myself to step back before I forget everything and kiss the hell out of her. First, I scan her accounts of their activities, then a list of encounters and kickbacks.

Seeing the Mayor's name, my head jerks in her direction. She nods and says, "There's more," but doesn't elaborate. That will be a question for later.

I turn, studying the maps even though I know Freedom like the back of my hand, having grown up there.

"Your plan is solid," I say, handing the legal pads to Cowboy, who has stepped up beside me. He is brutal in a fight like Hawk, but Cowboy has a head for planning and seeing outside the box. In the field, he always reviewed intel with me.

It only takes a few minutes of him looking over everything before he mumbles, "looks good," and steps back.

"Well, I'm glad you both approve," Gia says in a smart-ass tone, making me spin on her. I pull her into my arms and lower my face, so we are nose to nose.

"No one is second guessing or questioning you, Mi Alma. We work as a team. By that, I mean not us as Outcasts, but you and me," I growl out, so she knows how serious I am.

Her breathing picks up, and her hands fists the front of my t-shirt. Shit, she is aroused. The realization makes my dick go from comfortable to half-mass instantly.

"Why do you have schematics for a water tower on the wall?" Cowboy questions, jerking me out of my thoughts of carrying Gia into the nearest bedroom and seeing what the rest of her tastes like. I lick my lips and step back, releasing her.

My eyes go to the drawings Cowboy is pointing to. "That is a part of my long-term plan," Gia says with a shrug, looking at Cowboy, then she looks at me.

I raise a questioning eyebrow and wait.

"Ok, here's the cliff notes version. Do any of you know who actually owns Freedom? Not a building, not part of it, but the whole damn town?" she asks, and we all shake our heads no. It never crossed my mind that one person could own the whole damn thing.

"Well, let me explain some facts and see who guesses correctly. One day, Jose and Raphel go into Freedom, brutalize residents, destroy businesses, and the Wells City police refuse to do anything to help them," she pauses and shakes her head, anger rolling off her.

"Once they cleared out Freedom, the town was ripe for the taking. They start up a drug operation and open a brothel. Both are very lucrative. In a matter of days, all property in Freedom was sold," Gia walks to the table, picking up a stack of papers that look like copies of deeds and official records.

"Now, anyone wanna take a shot who bought it all and is making a very nice profit on kickbacks from the illegal activities there?"

Every muscle in my body goes rigid with this new information, and I grit my teeth." Wells City owns it, or is it the fucking Mayor himself?" I spit out the question burning in my mind.

"Wells City on the record, but all the money has gone into the mayor's pocket. Don't ask me how he has gotten everything past eight city council members. But I will tell you that it will be mine in 24 hours," she says with a cocky smirk on her face.

I relax my muscles and raise a questioning brow. "You're buying it?" I ask.

"Hell, no!" she says firmly, slamming the papers back down. "I'm taking it, or should I say he will willingly sign everything over to me. All of this," Gia says, pointing around at the maps and the table full of plans and notes.

"All of it is my plans for a new Freedom. A town run by its own laws, police force, legalized gambling within town limits, fire department, everything fully self-sufficient and functioning apart from Wells City by the time I'm finished with it," she says.

Gia's face is glowing with pride and determination. Bo walks to her side and throws an arm around her shoulder, grinning.

"We are going to build not just a home for people like us who don't fit into normal society or don't want to be a part of it. A town with Mayor Gia running it," Bo laughs, and Gia elbows him.

Mia, who has been quiet all this time, jumps up and throws her arm around Gia from the other side, grinning. "And I'm her new Town Planner."

I glance in Cowboy's direction, and his lip is twitching, trying his best not to smile.

Chapter 10

Gia

Everyone is quiet for a few minutes, taking in all the information I just threw at them. My plans will be a huge undertaking, but I straighten my shoulders. I've always hated my last name because of its association with my former father.

However, when Nonno was Don of the family, the D'Angelo name carried respect and honor even with his criminal activities. People knew he cared, and I want that for the future of what Freedom will be.

Bo Looks down at me with an understanding look. He and I have talked in detail about what my dream is. Hell, he probably knows what I'm thinking. "I'll unpack our goodies and get them loaded," he says, walking to the bags and unloading the guns and ammo we bought on our way home.

The Outcasts watch what he's doing, then start helping. Blaze takes me by the arm and guides me through the living room and into the bathroom, shutting the door.

I lean back on the wall opposite the vanity, waiting to hear what he says as my eyes take him all in.

From my view of his back, I can see his black t-shirt hugs his broad shoulders and muscular biceps. My eyes go lower to his tapered waist down to his round hard ass I bet you could bounce a quarter off of.

His body turns facing me just as I squeeze my thighs together, making heat rush to my face. Shit, did he notice? His lip twitches, and I know my answer.

Blaze leans forward, placing his forearms against the wall on each side of my head, caging me in. Those gorgeous brown eyes roam over my face. Then, he looks into my eyes, making my breath catch.

"I agree with your plan of two teams attacking simultaneously tonight. But I can't have you in danger," he says lowly, pressing his body into mine.

I inhale, and his warm, masculine scent envelops me. Damn, what does he shower with? Get out of your head, Gia, I scold myself.

"I'm perfectly capable of handling myself, Blaze. Don't you think I worry about you too?" I toss back at him.

He raises an eyebrow and pulls back slightly. "You don't have the training I do."

I lay my palms on his chest, feeling the body heat radiating off him. "That may be true, but make no mistake, the men my Nonno are sending will be the best," I say confidently.

I wouldn't be surprised if some of them were his personal security to ensure my safety.

"Promise me something," Blaze says, running his nose up my face. His warm breath caresses my skin light as a feather, making my nipples harden.

I run my hands down his chest and over his stomach. Feeling ripped abs beneath my fingertips as I slide my hands to his sides, gripping his waist. My panties are wet now, and my clit is begging for attention. "What do you want me to promise you?" I breathe out in a whisper.

"You will delegate letting them enter the Hotel ahead of you. Fuck Gia, I have to know you're safe, or I won't be able to keep my focus," he says low and deep.

My brain comes out of its lust-induced haze on hearing his words. Being separated with all these new feelings overwhelming us could be a major distraction. That's not good.

I push on his chest so that he looks me in the eye again. "You want to make demands, then I have a few of my own," I say firmly, watching his expression.

The muscles in his jaw flex, and his face looks serious. "Ok, what are they?" he asks.

"You want to be a part of my life? All of it? Then no hiding or pushing me away like you do, Big C," I say, seeing pain flash in his eyes, but it's gone as soon as it appeared.

"Ya, I know how you keep him at arm's length, and it's tearing him apart, Blaze. He loves you. So, fix that shit," I state firmly. I don't know Blaze's whole story, but he has a fantastic father he's hurting. It needs to stop. Blaze nods once, so I continue.

"As for me, I want a true partner. A man I can take all my pain, all my past shit, and lay it at his feet. Not so he can fix it, but because I trust him enough to be vulnerable and share those parts of myself. If a man can't do the same in return with me, then he's not a partner or soulmate, as you call me," I take a much-needed breath, but I'm not done. I'm laying it all out there on the line for him.

"You said you want to claim me as your woman. So, decide right now, Blaze, are you my partner and soulmate, or do you walk away?" I need to know now before my heart is fully invested.

I hold my breath, waiting for his response as he clenches his jaw tight and pushes off the wall away from me. He gives me one firm nod with a steeled look, then turns, jerking the bathroom door open, and walks out.

My chest feels like it's splitting in two as my eyes fill with tears. He fucking walked away. After everything he said, everything he made me feel, he walked out.

My lungs are tight, and I feel like I can't breathe. Stepping forward I grasp the vanity and force an inhale of air into them. It hurts. My chest hurts.

I furiously wipe the tears that escaped, running down my cheeks, and look in the mirror above the vanity. This isn't who I am. Staring into my reflection, I brace myself and square my shoulders. "No man will define me. Be you," I whisper and turn, walking into the living room.

The Outcasts are all filing out the door, leaving. Bo and Mia both look at me questioningly. I take a deep breath and tell it like it is.

"I laid everything out for him, my expectations and needs. He chose to walk," I say, refusing to shed another tear. Bo and Mia, both rush me, enveloping me in a group hug.

"Oh shit, oh shit," the man chirps, pacing on his perch.

"Fuck him, he isn't good enough for you," Mia says, squeezing me tightly.

"He's a dumb motherfucker if he lets you go," Bo says, then steps back, releasing me.

"Ya, well, I'm not going to dwell on it. We need to eat something and get ready," I say, trying to change the subject. I can't think about the fact I feel like someone just ripped my heart out of my chest.

"Kick his ass, kick his ass," the man screeches, but I ignore him.

Bo and Mia nod at me. I look at Mia and remember how we met. "Are you staying here or coming with us?" I have to ask because she may need more closure than she got two years ago.

I was riding my bike downtown Wells City, a few blocks from the old high school when I spotted three men next to a van trying to force a young woman into it.

She dropped her school books, screamed, and was struggling against them. Without conscious thought, I gunned the throttle and went off-road onto the sidewalk straight for them.

After running one down and wrecking my bike, I fought the other. Between Mia and I, as well as a few well-placed kicks to their groins and punches to the throat, we beat their asses.

Mia and I rode out of there relatively unharmed despite some bruises and my bike needing a new paint job. But neither of us has forgotten that Raphel's men tried to grab her.

I took Mia to the gym I trained at since she didn't want to go home, and our story went from there. She became my little sister and me her mentor.

As for Raphel, Bo and I caught him out one night after I heard he was behind Mia's attack. He was in the alley behind a strip club smoking. Bo and I worked him over pretty good, and he was warned to leave the girls in Wells City alone, or we would bury him.

Needless to say, no more girls went missing after that, but when I went to my then 'father' about what was going on, he told me to mind my business.

My gut clenches knowing what I know now. He has made money off of Raphel and everything he has done. It makes me feel sick.

"I'm going," Mia says, and I don't hear any hesitation.

"Ok, but you stay right beside me or Bo. Got it?" It's not a question. It's an order, and she knows it.

"Got it," she replies.

I nod and look at Bo. "Would you mind picking us up a pizza from down the street while we get changed?" I ask.

He smiles and kisses Mia and me on the head before walking out the door.

"He's a good brother," Mia says, and I laugh.

"He's the best," I reply, walking into my bedroom. Mia follows me in and watches me grab two pairs of black jeans and sweatshirts, throwing them onto the bed for us.

She has nothing right now, but we'll change that. "Are you a size 8 or 10?" I ask, looking her over.

She turns her head as if embarrassed. I step closer, taking her chin so she is looking right at me. Mia has curves like I do. Seeing her embarrassed because of that pisses me off.

"I don't care what anyone has told you. Women are supposed to have curves. Tits, ass, and thighs are sexy as hell to most men. But what's important is to own both who and what you are. If someone doesn't like it, well, then fuck them. Understand me?" I ask, but my voice is stern. I need her to hear what I'm saying.

Mia will be 18 in a matter of weeks. She is a 5 foot 6-inch curvy Latino woman with full breasts and an ass that most women would love to have. Her long dark hair and chocolate eyes only highlight her olive skin tone. She is gorgeous, and I would like to kick someone's ass for making her feel differently.

"I understand," she says with a sparkle in her eye, standing straighter. "I wear a size 12 jeans," she says proudly, and I laugh.

That's my girl own that shit. I walk back over to the closet and pull out a larger pair of jeans I wear on my 'oh my god, these cramps are going to kill me' days, and I need loose-fitting clothes.

I hand them to her, and she grins. We both change into black outfits and pin our long hair into buns. I nod at her when we're done.

Bo returns with pizza, and we all sit at the bar to eat. After finishing my second slice, I get up, getting us all bottles of water to wash it down.

"How is this going to work after tonight?" Bo says, and I look at him closely. He chooses his words carefully, and I realize what he's asking.

"You mean with things between Blaze and Me?" I ask to be sure, but my chest aches just thinking about him and how he walked out. I reach up, rubbing it without thought.

"The best thing to do since he has the bar in Freedom is to act like nothing happened. I will own the building he's in. So, a tenant-landlord professional relationship. Everything will be business, and he will only have as much say in town matters as any other resident who wants to live there," I state, hating to hear those words, but it's how it will have to be.

"I had thought of using the Outcast as the police force, but that's out of the question now," I gather my thoughts and look to Mia.

"Tomorrow, look into security companies. For now, I will hire someone to help protect our town and us. At least until we find the right people," I tell her, and she nods, grabbing a note pad writing it down.

I look at Bo, who is grinning at me. The man has a serious thing for bossy women. "You still want to set up and run the warehouse we're building. Overseeing the fights and gambling?" I ask him.

"Hell yes, you know that's my dream," he replies.

I grin, knowing he will be amazing at it. You wouldn't know it by looking at Bo or watching him fight, but his abilities with numbers are crazy. He's like a human calculator with mad fighting skills.

"That will be the primary income for the town, so I'm counting on you," Bo sits straighter and gets a cocky smirk.

"When have I ever let you down?" he asks, and I shake my head.

"Never, and I know you won't. Besides, it's not like we're broke," I say with a wicked grin. But I'm not stupid. I may be a millionaire now, but that money won't last forever if I'm not smart.

My goal is to make Freedom profitable within six months. Until then, I will be careful about how it's spent.

We sit and discuss both the attack and our plans until there is a knock at the door. I stand, slipping my Glock into my thigh holster, and answer it.

When I see it's Sammy, my Nonno's main guard, with 19 other men I've seen over the years, I step aside, allowing them in.

They walk around assessing the apartment, then quietly gather in the dining room, looking at the maps. I walk over, and they make way for me to get to the maps.

Taking my time, I walk them through the plans, pointing to each building and where they post men as lookouts at night.

They talk amongst themselves for a minute before I continue with the plan. Once I am finished with what I want, Sammy steps forward.

"We brought a cargo van for disposal later. But how do you want the women dealt with after we take Raphael and his men out?" he asks.

"They will be forced out of town and warned never to return. I want everyone gone so I can start with a clean slate with Freedom," I say firmly.

Sammy nods, stepping back. I look at the clock on the microwave, reading 3:15 am.

"Let's go," I order, grabbing a second-loaded Glock off the bar and sticking it in the back of my jeans. Bo does the same, and we march downstairs to our bikes.

Mia stands looking between Bo and me, and I smile. "Get on."

Once we mount up and Mia is holding on tight, we start the engines and roll out of the parking lot with four black SUVs and a cargo van following us.

That's not conspicuous at all, right?

Chapter 11

Blaze

Hearing Gia's words as she laid out what she needed set a fire ablaze in me. She deserves everything she said and much more.

I need to wrap my head around telling her everything. Fuck, losing her isn't an option. She is everything I have ever wanted. Her words repeat in my head; I need to get my shit straight.

I stare into those beautiful eyes of Gia's, which will forever be my home. I know what I have to do. Pushing myself off the wall, I turn and walk out of the bathroom on a mission.

Finding pops and setting things right with him before we attack tonight. I should have talked to him sooner instead of being an asshole son.

Then after we deal with shit in Freedom, I'll show her my demons. Will she still want me, then?

Walking through the living room with determination, I barely notice all heads turning towards me. I ignore them all. I have one goal in mind: seeing Pop and fixing the mess I created with our relationship.

"Blaze, wait up, man," Cowboy's voice rings out behind me, and I pause, sitting on my bike as my brothers gather around.

"You've got to talk to us," he says, crossing his arms over his chest and narrowing his eyes at me, waiting.

These are my brothers, and with the shit we've been through together, they'll get what I'm about to say. "I need to set things right with Pops before we deal with the shit in Freedom," I say, looking each of my brothers in the eye.

A few grunts and some nods of understanding sound out.

"So, Rebel talked some sense into you?" Cowboy asks with a chuckle.

I look back at him and smirk. "I guess you could say that. I need you guys to head back to the bar and round up the prospects and artillery we'll need. I'll meet you back there after I talk with Pop," I say, starting the engine.

A unanimous "Hooyah" rings out as they disperse, climbing on their bikes. I back out of the parking spot and roll the throttle, heading to Pop's place.

When I arrive at his apartment and knock, my nerves feel rattled. I have led men into enemy camps armed to the teeth without a second thought but talking about feelings and shit is hard.

Pop opens the door with a surprised expression when he sees me. "Angel, everything ok?"

I don't know where to start as I stand here looking at the man who has raised and loved me—a man who deserves to be treated better.

With no words, I step forward and embrace him. "Missed you, Pop," my voice coming out gravelly.

He returns the hug, slapping my back. "Missed you too," he choked out. Shit, the only time I've ever seen Pop's shed a tear is at Madre's grave.

I slap his back in return before we pull back. "Want some coffee?" Pop asks, and I nod.

I sit at the table while he pours two cups and sits across from me. He studies my face before taking a drink. "You in on this Freedom plan Gia told me about?"

His question doesn't come across as judgmental, just curious. I nod in reply.

"Be safe," he says, then works his jaw like he does when in deep thought. I'm sure he's wondering why I'm here or what's changed.

I clear my throat and start talking. "I've been a shit son since I came back," I say, meeting his gaze, and he nods.

"Some things happened my last few months that changed me. Changed me in ways I can't come back from," I pause, taking a drink, but Pop doesn't say a word, just keeps studying my face. I don't miss the sadness in his eyes, though.

"I stupidly thought that keeping you at arm's length would protect you from the darkness in here," I point to my head, and Pop starts shaking his head, but I continue.

"The fear of you being able to accept who I am now played a part in it, too. But that's on me, Pop's not you. You've always been there, and I'm sorry," as soon as the words leave my mouth, Pop is out of his seat and at my side.

I stand, and his arms jerk me to him in a crushing embrace. "I've seen men come back just fine but stronger. I've also seen men come back with demons that haunt them. Make no mistake, Angel, nothing in this world could change my love for you or how proud I am of the man you are."

I grasp the back of his shirt, balling it into my fist, willing the tears rising to go away as I squeeze my eyes shut.

"I love you," he says, slapping my back and pulling away too soon. It's been years since we've had a moment like this.

"Love you too, Pop's," I reply, retaking my seat. We quietly drink our coffee before he speaks again.

"So, you and Gia?" he asks with a half-smile and a knowing look.

I return his smile and nod. "I'll claim her as mine after we deal with Freedom," I reply firmly.

"You'll have your hands full with that one, but I approve," he says, chuckling.

"I'm sure I will," I laugh. "Why do they call her Rebel?" I ask, curious.

Pop leans back in his chair with a grin. "That one hates orders and authority. Tell her to do something, and she'll do the opposite to spite you."

I smile at that. "So, she won't jump off a bridge if you tell her to," I say jokingly and swallow the last of my coffee, thinking about my woman.

"Hell no, she would throw you off and walk away laughing," he says, shaking his head.

I, on the other hand, burst with laughter at the thought. My mafia princess is a little badass. Then it hit me how she reacted when I called her princess at the bar, and my stomach tightened.

I can't wait to learn everything about her, but one thing is sure: I'll never call her that again.

Glancing at my watch, I see it's close to time and stand.

Pop comes around the table with a worried look. "Don't be a stranger anymore," he says.

"Those days are over, Pop's. As soon as things settle down, we'll have dinner," I say, and he nods.

The cool early morning air bites at my skin as I roar under the overpass into Freedom. Pulling into my bar, I see the old van we usually keep out back being loaded with guns and ammo by the prospects. They give me chin jerks in respect as I park.

Walking inside with sure steps, I scan the bar, seeing my brothers in full tactical gear loading themselves with extra clips. When my eyes flick to the table they are around, I see grenades in the center.

"What the fuck are you thinking?" I ask, picking one up and looking at each of them.

"Thought we should take some just in case," Hawk shrugs.

I shake my head at him. "We're taking out the trash, not burning shit down," I say, putting it back on the table.

"Hunter, take ten prospects and Hawk to the back entrance," I say, tossing him the keys to the van Axel converted to a mobility van for Hunter. "Come straight back for us."

Then, looking at Hawk, I order, "You're leading them, but don't breach or engage until I give the signal."

Hawk grins, grabbing his guns and heading for the door behind Hunter.

I turn towards Cowboy, who hands me a tactical vest, and I slip it on. The familiar calmness washes over me. The deadly calm that I'm all too familiar with from missions.

"We'll meet Gia and Bo at the Townline. Everyone ready for this?" I ask, looking around at my brothers and the remaining prospects that have trickled in from outside.

"Hooyah," rings out, and I feel pride in my men. My brothers.

"Once we breach the complex, we will clear it floor by floor, starting from the ground and working our way up. You two," I say, pointing to two prospects. "Go with Cowboy to take out their lookouts. Do it silently."

I hear the van pulling in for us and put two more clips in my vest. "Load up," I order, turning and marching towards the door.

We arrive at the town line, and Hunter pulls off the road next to the old wooden sign that has seen better days. I exit the passenger side and walk around to Hunter's window, waiting for Gia, Bo, and her men to arrive.

The cool morning air feels thick, and the anticipation of seeing my woman rises as I stare down the road, waiting. It isn't long until I faintly see SUVs approaching in the distance, and I smile.

The first SUV comes to a stop, and the window lowers. A man I have seen with Gia's Nonno is driving with Gia in the passenger seat.

She turns towards me, and my pulse picks up at seeing her beautiful face. But when I take in her expression, my gut tightens.

"You and the Outcasts ready?" she asks, emotionless. What the fuck is going on?

"We're always ready," I reply.

"Let's do it then," she says, and the window goes up, and they drive away, leaving me confused as hell.

Has something happened? I shake my head because we have to do this simultaneously so one can't warn the other.

I jog over to the van and jump in.

84

"Everything ok?" Hunter asks.

I hit the dash twice, not looking at him. "Let's roll out," I order, grinding my teeth together. I'll figure it out later; right now, I need my head straight.

We quietly roll through town, circling behind the apartment complex that Jose and his men are in. All the emotions boil up inside me with thoughts of how they terrorized this town, attacked residents, and destroyed businesses along with my Pop's gym.

I spot our men in the alleyway waiting for my signal; rolling down the window, I whistle, and they jump into action as Hunter parks the van.

We all exit with purpose. Our steps are silent as we reach the front of the complex. The tension in the air is heavy like a storm cloud as I draw my weapon and breach the front entrance.

With a nod to my men, we fan out into the shadows with precision. Working together for years has made us a well-oiled machine with sharp eyes.

My heart pounding in my chest as the first shots ring out. Hearing the motor on the elevator, I swiftly turn and nod at Cowboy to watch my six as I make my way toward it. The stairway entrance and elevator are side by side. They are trapped like rats in a cage with only two ways down here.

I silently motion for five prospects to go with Hawk up the stairwell to clear the next floor while Cowboy and the rest of the men wait for the elevator doors to open.

With half of us on each side of it, our guns were drawn as the doors opened. Immediately, the smell of gunpowder invades my nostrils as shots ring out.

Three men drop to the floor as we return fire, hitting our marks. Once we check for pulses, I jam my knife into the door, forcing it to stay open and putting the elevator out of use.

We all rush up the stairs, passing the second floor since Hawk and the Men have it covered, and go to the third floor.

Opening the door, we exit two by two, alternating going left and right as we clear each apartment. Finding them all empty, I realize that when Jose's men heard our gunshots, they must have gone up to protect him.

I turn to Cowboy without a word and point to the ceiling, indicating they went up. He nods, and we go up to the 4th floor, meeting Hawk and the prospects there.

The apartment doors are open, indicating they left in a rush. However, one door at the end of the corridor is shut.

I slide a fresh clip out of my vest while simultaneously ejecting the one from my gun. Slapping in the new clip, I nod, and Hawk kicks the door in. We all step to the side as shots ring out.

Bullet holes riddle the hallway walls, and smoke fills the air. We charge in once they pause to reload, never missing a step as we take down every man in sight.

For several minutes, things move in slow motion as the chaos erupts; the sounds of our shots ringing out are deafening in the confined space.

I spot Jose standing tall in the back of the room, but his eyes, which generally look cold, now show defeat. His gaze fixes on me with pure hatred, and I grin.

Just as he raises his arm, I see a glint of metal in his hand and fire before he can pull the trigger.

His face turns to shock, and his eyes widen as he drops to his knees. I fire a second round, hitting him between the eyes for good measure.

I turn, assessing all of my men. "Anyone hit or injured?" I yell out.

They all look at each other, shaking their heads. When my eyes lock with Kane, I see recognition in his eyes. Losing Tommy on our last mission changed us. The thought of losing another man makes my chest tighten.

I shake those thoughts, knowing I need to check on my woman now that Jose is out of the way.

She could be in danger right now rings out in my head. I rush towards the door. "Let's give Gia and Bo backup," I call over my shoulder, taking the steps two at a time.

Once outside, we pile into the van, knowing Hunter will have to come back for the prospects.

As soon as I shut my door, I turn to Hunter, "Floor it; Gia may need us," I order.

When Cowboy gets the side door closed, Hunter does just that, lurching us forward. Bracing myself with the dash as we race towards her, my stomach is in knots.

I need to see her, touch her, know that she's ok.

Chapter 12

Gia

With my back to the wall and my pulse pounding in my ears, I grip my Glock tighter. Nodding to Bo, we both turn the knob to the last room on the top floor of the hotel.

Women are huddled against the far wall of a bedroom. I quickly scan the room with my gun raised, but they're alone.

Then, I take in my surroundings. A mattress is on the floor with one pillow and an old comforter. Clothes are strewn on the floor, and a chest of drawers is in the corner. Nothing else. These women have been living like this?

I shake my head and lower my gun, seeing they're scared.

Sammy comes in and stops beside me. "The rest of the floor is clear," he says, but his eyes are on the women.

I nod and then look back at the prostitutes. Are they here willingly?

"Get dressed, and you will be escorted downstairs," I said, turning.

Georgio is in the hallway waiting for us. "Bring them downstairs when they finish," I say, walking past, and he nods.

We still haven't found Raphel, and I know he's here. He is always here at this hour. I raise my weapon as Bo and Sammy walk past me and start down the stairs.

We silently make our way to the main level of the hotel. One of Nonno's men is at the end of a dark hallway and gives a head jerk. Indicating there is someone in a back office.

The door to the office is slightly ajar, with a soft glow from a lamp pouring through. I hear rustling and low cursing. Knowing we already took out all his men, this must be Raphel.

I step forward past Sammy and Bo, easing the door open further. Raphel is frantically emptying a large old safe. What a fucking coward. He was going to run.

Aiming my gun at him and chuckling menacingly, he turns towards me, dropping the bundles of cash in his hands.

He raises them slowly with a shocked expression. Seeing his Adam's apple slowly bob, indicating a hard swallow. Good, he should be scared.

"Sit," I order. Raphel shakes his head as his eyes look at each of us.

Sammy takes two long strides, grabbing him by the throat and forcing him into an armchair. Raphel opens his mouth to speak, but Sammy punches him so hard in the jaw his head whips to the side, nearly tipping the chair over.

Damn, he can pack a punch.

"If I, were you, I would keep my mouth shut unless told to speak," I say, laughing.

Keeping my gun aimed at him, I look around the office. There is money on the desk and floor. Ledgers are open on the desk, and my feet move on their own accord, taking me closer.

I scan the columns of numbers and dates. Wednesdays, Fridays, and Sundays show regular money in, but Mondays payments out. The mayor, Anthony D'Angelo, and 'D' are in parenthesis—my head jerks towards Raphel.

Georgio comes in, getting our attention. "We have the women together in the lobby. Otherwise, the hotel is clear."

"How many?" I ask.

"9," Georgio replies.

"Bring them in here," I say, holstering my gun and leaning against the desk. I glance over at Raphel, who sits nervously while Sammy has a hand on his shoulder in a brutal grip, keeping him seated.

The women enter the office, their eyes darting around as they cling to each other. Some are sniffling and crying, which isn't surprising. Armed men just came in, taking down this whole operation. Not to mention, there are still dead bodies lying around.

I look them over carefully. "Are any of you here against your will?" I ask. Knowing Raphel's past reputation before Bo and I warned him.

The eldest of the women steps forward. She is probably in her early 30s. "No, those girls were sold to the Diablo's. They were never here longer than 24 hours," she says.

Rage. White hot rage boils up inside me as I look over at Raphel. Selling young girls. The mayor and my former father were profiting from human trafficking.

I feel bile rising, and my stomach turns at the thought. I swallow hard and try to get myself under control.

"Here's what's going to happen," I say, pointing to the corner of the room where a black duffle bag lays on the floor.

"Grab that bag and take this money," I say, gesturing to the mess on the floor and desk.

I look at Raphel as he opens his filthy mouth again to argue, and he quickly clamps his lips closed. "Give me your keys," I order.

He reaches into his pants, pulling out a set of keys, and I turn, handing them to the older woman.

"You all take the money, leave town, preferably the state. You will never come back," I say firmly with a raised brow.

She nods frantically with the other women as they start scooping money up and stuffing it into the duffle bag.

"You never seen us, and this night never happened. Understood?" I say, standing straight and squaring my shoulders.

"Yes," they say, taking the money and keys, hurrying out the door, and leaving.

"Georgio, make sure they leave freedom," Sammy orders him. Then Sammy turns his attention to me.

"What about Raphel?" he asks.

I stare down at the disgusting man in the chair. There needs to be a special place in hell for men like him. I'll send him there for all he has done, but first, he will learn a hard lesson here. Women are not commodities to be used.

I step beside Raphel but keep my eyes on Sammy. Throwing my thumb over my shoulder as I speak. "Take a look," I say, and Sammy's eyes flicker to the desk before he walks over.

His eyes scan the ledgers as I watch different emotions cross his face. Sammy's face goes red, his head jerks up, and his eyes bore into mine with the same realization I had minutes ago.

"Let me be the one who tells him."

Sammy clenches his jaw but nods his agreement.

"You got any chains or rope?" I ask.

He grins and walks out. Raphel leans forward like he will stand or make a run for it, so I grab him with both hands by the head, bringing my knee up.

The sickening sound of his nose breaking against my knee is satisfying. He screams out as his head flies backward. His hands go to his face, clutching it.

"You fucking bitch," he roars, lowering his hands, revealing a bloody nose and mouth.

I laugh at him. "You have no idea, but you will soon enough." He will find out what this bitch is capable of.

Sammy comes back carrying a bundle of rope, looking from the mess that is Raphel and then to me with a raised brow. I shrug and take the rope from him.

I step back once I have Raphel securely bound from his shoulders down to his feet. "Take him to the basement. I'll deal with him later," I say.

Sammy and two other men lift him, carrying him out, and I turn to the desk. Picking up the ledgers and other papers, I walk to the enormous safe that's taller than me. Shit, you could store bodies in here. Is this an old bank safe?

I see a shelf at the top and place everything on it. My eyes catch sight of something black. Reaching in, I feel hard plastic and pull it out. It's an old VHS tape. I flip it over, and a white label reads 'insurance.'

Humm. Whatever is on this has to be good. I place it back inside and walk into the lobby, where Bo and Mia are talking. "Everything good out here? And where have you been?" I ask.

"Ya were just waiting to see what's next. And I had some guys run me back to the apartment. Our bikes are here," Bo replies with a grin.

"Thanks. The contractor will be here at 8 am," I say, sliding the phone out of my pocket to see the time. It's 30 minutes from now.

Sammy and the men enter the lobby, and we walk outside with them. "I appreciate all your help. Tell Nonno I'll call him later," I tell Sammy with a smile.

He has been at my Nonno side since my earliest childhood memories. If I remember correctly, he even gave me a piggyback ride once or twice when I was little.

"Anytime you need us, call," Sammy says, and then they all load up into the SUVs after tossing the last of the bodies in the back.

As I watch them pull out of the parking lot, which has cracks and grass growing through in spots, I see an old van barreling up the road.

Shit, it's the Outcasts. I don't feel like dealing with Blaze right now. Not after he walked away. I'm happy to see he's okay, but I need to clear my head and think before talking to him. My chest hurts at just the thought of seeing him.

I turn, seeing where Bo has our bikes parked, and I jog over to mine, jumping on and starting it up.

"Where are you going?" Bo yells over the rumble of my bike.

"I need to clear my head," I yell over my shoulder as I back it up.

"The contractor," He yells back.

"Be back in 30," I reply, getting on the throttle and flying out of the parking lot as Blaze and the other Outcasts jump out of the van. Shit, I need to get myself together. My heart was more invested in him or us than I thought.

For days, I dreamt of a solid, loving relationship like Nonno and Nonna had. A man who would love and stand beside me no matter what. Damn, and the way he sets me on fire when he touches me.

No, Gia, stop thinking of all that. Get your head straight. I roll the throttle harder, feeling the cool morning air rush over me, whipping my hair all around.

A horn blaring catches my attention, and I look in my side mirror. Shit, their van is behind me and closing in fast. Fuck this, I roll the throttle more, and the front end rises slightly, making me lean forward, holding on tight.

Whoever is driving floors it and comes up beside me. I look over, and Blaze is rolling the passenger window down. "Pull the fuck over," he yells.

"Screw you," I replied, turning to see the old grocery store up ahead. I'll circle through their parking lot and head back. I have to meet this contractor.

I let off the throttle enough that I won't miss turning in, but they use that to their advantage, getting in front of me and stopping with the van sideways, blocking me.

Shit, what does he have to say that it can't wait? He made his feelings clear when he walked out on me.

I get on the brakes hard, forcing my back end to slide around on me. Once I come to a stop, I'm pissed off, and my heart is pounding. I toe the kickstand down and jump off the bike as Blaze jumps out of the van and comes charging towards me like a Mack truck.

"What the fuck are you doing taking off like that?" He yells as he gets close.

"What the hell are you doing chasing after me?" I retort. He is toe-to-toe with me and in my face by this time.

Blaze grabs me by the waist, pulling me to him. His arms are like steel bands trying to crush me. "You're mine, Gia. Been mine since I laid eyes on you. So, I'll ask again, what the fuck are you doing?" His eyes are searching mine for answers, and his jaw is flexing.

I place both my palms firmly on his chest, pushing him back hard. "You fucking walked away. I laid everything out and told you what I needed, and you chose to walk. So, keep on walking," I say, nearly choking on every word. But my heart can't take this. He needs to leave me alone.

His hand comes up, gripping the back of my head and a hand full of hair. "Fuck Gia, I didn't walk away from you," he shakes his head, and his face looks determined.

"Everything you said to me was true. I needed to get my shit straight and talk to Pop. I would never leave you, Gia. You are everything I have ever wanted. My other half, woman," his face is nearly touching mine now.

My chest feels like it's going to split into at his words. "You walked without a word, no nothing. You can't fucking do that," I say, clutching two fist full of his leather cut.

"Shit!" he says, realizing what I have been thinking and going through. "I've never been in a long-term relationship. I may fuck up sometimes, Gia, but us," he pauses, searching my face and holding me tighter. "We're forever."

I feel tears threatening to come. "You can't walk away, Blaze, never. We may argue, yell, or even break shit. But you can't ever walk out on me. Understand?"

That sexy smile of his spreads on his face, making my heartbeat pick up and my nipples pebble.

Blaze leans forward, running his nose along the side of my face to my ear, and goosebumps rise on my arms.

He nibbles on my earlobe, and I hear that deep baritone voice. "No walking away. But I won't promise what else I might do to you when I want my way."

He shifts his hips forward, rocking his hard bulge against my stomach, and he growls low and deep.

A whimper escapes me as my core pulses with need, and my panties dampen.

He pulls back enough to capture my lips with his. Every movement is slow and deliberate as he takes my mouth. His tongue pushes past my lips, and I gladly let him in. Wrapping my arms around his neck and pulling him closer, he reaches down, cupping my ass with his large hands.

He firmly squeezes a cheek in each hand and lifts me. I instinctively wrap my legs around his waist and grind myself into him.

The deep groan he releases into my mouth as he thrusts himself firmly against my core only fuels me more.

"Honk, Honk," the loud horn of the van blaring jerks us out of our heated make out session.

"As hot as that is to watch, we should all get out of the road," the man I now realize is Hunter yells at us, laughing.

I feel the heat rising to my cheeks, knowing he has been watching us dry hump each other in the street. Blaze chuckles and slaps my ass. The sting of it causes my core and legs to clench, and he raises an eyebrow at me.

"Does my Mi Alma like it a little rough?" he asks lowly.

"I don't know," I whisper. But damn, I'm up for finding out.

Blaze leans forward, giving me a gentle kiss before pulling away. "We will be exploring that very soon," he says, sitting me down next to my bike.

"I have to get back to meet the contractor, but we all need to have a long talk after," I say, looking at him.

Blaze nods, then turns towards Hunter. "Follow us back."

What does he mean by that?

Blaze steps around me and straddles my bike. "Get on, Gia," he says with a wicked grin.

I've never ridden with a man but the thought of wrapping myself around Blaze as we speed down the road is exhilarating. Besides, I can think of a few ways to keep my hands busy while he's driving, like exploring that sexy body of his.

I smile back and jump on behind him. He starts the engine, and I lean forward. "I hope you're not ticklish," I say as I reach around, running my hands from his sides up to his chest, then slowly down to his abs. Savoring every flex, ripple, and rugged ridge as I go.

His deep chuckle rings out into the air as we take off back to the hotel.

Chapter 13

Blaze

I don't know if I'm in heaven or hell the way Gia is torturing me. I'm finally at the point of snapping when I reach up, grab one of her hands, and hold it firmly in place on my stomach.

She has been exploring my chest, abdomen, and thighs the entire ride back, making me hard as a rock. When the Hotel comes into view, I exhale slowly, release her hand, and grasp the handlebars, turning in.

After I park, I dismount and lift her off, holding her soft, curvy body to mine. "Damn, woman, you like playing with fire."

"Maybe I want to get burned," she says with a sly smile, wrapping her arms around my waist and pressing that sexy body of hers into me.

I grind my throbbing hard cock into her and growl. "I'm going to do more than burn you, Mi Alma." (My soul)

Crashing my lips onto hers, I thread my fingers into her long hair and take control of the kiss. Pushing my tongue into her warm, wet mouth, I devour hers.

"I hate to interrupt you, love birds, but I'm on a schedule," a deep voice I don't recognize says. We pull away, and Gia leans her head against my chest to catch her breath while I look towards the Hotel.

My brothers and prospects are on the porch, trying to hide their smiles and laughter. But what caught my attention was two men I didn't recognize standing with Bo and Mia at the foot of the steps. The contractors, maybe?

Gia pulls away from me, but I don't let her go far. Keeping my arm firmly around her waist, we walk together to greet them. She is mine, and every damn man will know it.

"I'm Gia D'Angelo," she says, outstretching her hand to greet the older man, and I grit my teeth. I don't want her touching any man except me and fuck that last name. Soon, she will be carrying mine.

They shake, and he chuckles. "I'm Sal, and I'm well aware of who you are. Your Nonno and I go way back," he says.

"I was told you are both skilled and have a unique quality," Gia retorts, tilting her head to the side with a grin. I tighten my hold on her, wondering what she's talking about.

"Oh Ya, what did your Nonno say about me?" he raises a brow.

"That you are discrete," Gia says, widening her smile.

"Humm, that I am. Shall we get started on a walk-through while you explain your needs?" he asks, turning to look at the front of the Hotel, then he glances around the parking lot.

"Sure," Gia replies.

"I'm assuming a fresh coat of paint and parking lot repair is on the list," he murmurs, taking in the peeling paint on the Hotel and grass growing up through cracks in the parking lot.

"Yes," Gia replies and wraps her arm around my waist, making me smile as we enter the Hotel. Mia and Bo follow closely behind us. Mia is carrying folders and a legal pad while Bo is carrying that damn bank bag. What is it with these two walking around with loads of cash like it's normal?

"Would you prefer to do this room by room or for me to list the changes and updates I want?" Gia asks as we stop in the middle of the lobby.

"I can make a list if that helps," Mia says, stepping beside us with a pen ready to write. I grin at her. Gia made the right choice, putting her in the position of town planner. Mia may be young, but she is eager and intelligent.

"I want carpet removed throughout, plumbing and electrical checked, vanities, showers, toilets, and locks replaced," Gia says, then pauses, looking around.

She pulls away from me, and I reluctantly let her go, but I stay close. Following her to the long wooden counter meant for the desk clerks to stand behind, she runs her hand over the smooth oak with a smile.

"Leave this," she says, then pointing at the wall of boxed shelves behind it meant for keys and messages.

"I want those gone and a mirror and new shelving for liquor bottles in its place."

"You're turning the hotel into a bar?" Sal asks, stepping close with a curious look. His closeness kicks my protective instincts into gear, and I wrap my arm around Gia again.

When she leans into me, I relax my muscles.

"Sal, this isn't going to be a bar or a hotel. This," she says, gesturing around with her hand. "This is going to be my home. Our home," she grips my arm around her waist and looks around the lobby at my brothers and prospects.

The surprised look on their faces, I'm sure, matches my own, and I tighten my hold on her. She tilts her head back, looking at me. "We're going to be a family. Am I correct that you have been using the bar for meetings but having to live separately?" she asks.

We haven't had the time or money to set up a proper clubhouse as a newly formed MC, and we have only been out of the military for a short time. I nod in reply.

"Well, we're going to be family, partners. The Grand Hotel has 30 rooms, all with ensuites and balcony access. More than enough for everyone," she grins up at me, and I hear a few hoots and hollers from my brothers, making me chuckle.

"Not to break up the party, but as I said, I'm on a schedule," Sal says, gaining our attention.

"Besides what I have listed, you can do any repairs you find. There is a matter of something special I need," Gia says, and Sal's spine straightens.

She leads me to the right down the hall past offices, stopping at the only door on the left. Gia turns, looking at Sal, "I want this door to the basement hidden, then I need a unique build in the basement." She opens the door, and we descend a wide wooden staircase.

At the bottom, we stop, and I am amazed at the open space. The basement must span the entire hotel floor plan. It's open with only pillars for support every so often. Groaning gets my attention, and everyone turns, seeing Raphel hog-tied near the wall. I grin but look towards Sal, wondering how he will react.

To my surprise, he showed no acknowledgment and looked back at us to continue. Why the hell is she keeping Raphel alive?

Gia pulls out of my arms and heads to the back wall. I follow along side of Sal. She stops 30 feet from the back.

"I need a wall with a door separating this back section, and Mia can give you specs for the unique build that goes inside."

Mia steps up, handing Sal a printout, and I lean closer. It's for a fucking crematorium with double burners. My head jerks up, looking at Gia. She gives me a mischievous smirk. I know I shouldn't be surprised by anything knowing who her family is but damn.

She walks over, wrapping her arms around my waist, and I embrace her. If we run into trouble, disposal won't be an issue.

"I'm assuming you don't want us to just buy and install this because of the attention it would bring?" Sal asks, his gaze going from the schematics to Gia.

"That's correct. However, if it's built from those, no one is the wiser," she grins.

Sal smiles and nods. "What else?" he asks.

"There is also the matter of two urgent new builds that need to stay under the radar until complete," Gia says. Why does it need to be kept quiet? I look down at her, confused.

Mia hands Sal two more printouts with notes on them, and he looks over them.

"A water tower with a filtration system and a Warehouse?" He asks questioningly.

"That's right. Kits for both are in stock over in Billsby. Your men would do assembly," she says with confidence.

Sal's eyes roam the basement, but his expression says he is in deep thought. "How fast of a turnaround do you need?" he asks, looking back at us.

"A week," Gia says, and Sal throws his head back, laughing.

Once he catches his breath, he looks at her with amusement. "No matter what people may think, I can't just snap my fingers, and things magically happen, young lady."

His sarcastic tone makes me stiffen, and I'm ready to throw him the fuck out. Gia tightened her hold on my arms around her, and I tried to relax some. If she wants to handle this, I'll try to let her.

To my surprise, she gets a cocky look on her face and tilts her head to the side. "Sal, how big is your operation?"

He raises a brow but answers. "I have 150 employees, 119 of which are on working crews."

Gia nods, and her smile widens. "Are you a betting man, Sal?"

Sal's lip twitches at that question, and his eyes sparkle. "I've been known to place a bet or two," he replies.

Gia nods and leans forward, her face showing amusement. "I'd be willing to bet that a $200k bonus to you on top of your normal rate at the end of the week could ensure that you and your men have these three projects completed to my satisfaction," she says with bravado, making me chuckle.

Bo and Mia both smile and turn away, trying to hide them.

Sal laughs a deep belly laugh while shaking his head. "You are just like your Nonno. Yes, I can make that happen by delaying some other jobs," he says.

"Good," Mia replies, leaning back into me. I guess that means we will all be moving into the Hotel next week. I shake my head. Our home, it won't be a hotel anymore.

Once we all return to the lobby, Sal and his man look towards the upstairs grand staircase. "Are the rooms empty?" he asks, not bothering to look back at us.

"No, but they will be," Gia replies, tilting her head back and looking at me, and I know what she's thinking. We will help. Shit, this is going to be our home, I'll put the prospects to work. I nod down at her that I'll take care of it.

"I'll be here with the crew in the morning. Dumpsters will be delivered out front by this afternoon. Any specifics on fixtures for the bathrooms you want to be redone?" he asks, finally turning toward us.

"Modern and clean. Otherwise, no. I'm not picky," she replies, and he nods back.

"Anything we're forgetting?" he says with a thoughtful look.

"Oh shit, yes," Gia says, standing straight. "Do you know anyone who can reset an old safe combination with a new one?" she asks him excitedly.

Sal grins at her. "How old are we talking?"

"Older than dirt, big enough to store bodies in. It looks like an old bank safe and says Wells Fargo on it," she rambles, making us all chuckle.

"My cousin Vinny has a security company. I can have him come take a look," Sal says, and Gia nods.

After Sal and his man leave, Gia sighs loudly, turning to face me. "I know you have many questions, and we need to discuss things. Can we get some food, and all go to the bar?" she asks.

Damn, this woman is everything. I step forward and embrace her. "Yes, I'll send a few prospects for food while we talk," I say, leaning my forehead against hers. I could get lost staring into those big brown eyes and her soft coconut scent.

"I have a few questions of my own," Cowboy speaks up, and there are several murmurs of agreement as Gia and I turn, facing everyone staring at us.

"I need three prospects on a breakfast run. Everyone else loads up for the first Freedom Town meeting at Angel's," I announce firmly.

Several prospects head for the exit, and we follow behind. I get on when we reach her bike, but Gia pauses, looking back at the Hotel. "Home," she whispers, but I hear her. Has she ever really had a home? The question comes out of nowhere in my mind, making my stomach tighten.

Chapter 14

Gia

Walking into the bar, Blaze takes my hand in his large one, and calmness flows through me from the raw power radiating off him. Bo and I aren't doing this all on our own.

I smile, thinking of how large our group is getting, our family. If we work as a team, making Freedom into the town I have dreamed of for years will be a reality sooner than I thought.

Blaze squeezes my hand, and I look up at him as we walk through the bar. "What has you smiling, Mi Alma?" (My soul)

Those handsome brown eyes of his sparkle down at me. Damn, this man knows how to make me weak in the knees with just a look.

"I was just thinking how much easier it's going to be making my dream a reality with us all working together," I say.

Blaze leads me to a back table, then pulls me onto his lap, wrapping his arms around me in a warm embrace. I inhale, taking in his warm, masculine scent that is uniquely him, and he grins down at me mischievously. What is he up to?

I soon find out when he looks around the room with a serious expression. "Prospects, I want Freedom on lockdown for the next week. No one gets in unless they are a construction crew member or are delivering supplies or equipment for them. Got it?" Blaze's voice rings out, echoing off the walls.

The prospects all start talking amongst themselves about patrols and shifts.

"Move out," Cowboy's voice is deep and commanding, making the prospects all head for the door. The vibration of Blaze's laughter beneath me makes it hard to hide my smile.

Bo, Mia, and the officers of the Outcasts all gather around us, taking seats. My body melts into Blaze as he cradles my back firmly to his chest.

"Coffee's on Pres," Hunter says, rolling over to join us. This is the first time I have looked at him. It must be tough going from being an elite military man to being in a wheelchair. Then it hit me: the hotel has an elevator, but I didn't see a ramp outside.

As others begin to talk around me, I ignore them, sliding my phone from my pocket and texting Nonno. "What's Sal's number?"

He replies shortly with his number, making me smile. "Thanks. Ti Amo," (love you) I reply.

Then, I quickly send a message to Sal, adding a wheelchair ramp to the front and back porches of the hotel. His reply was abrupt, no doubt, because I added more to his workload, making me snicker. But I will make sure every member of our new family is comfortable. That means access for Hunter.

I put my phone away, looking back at him. To my surprise, Hunter is already looking at Blaze and me with amusement. "What's so funny?" I ask him.

"The fact that a sweet thing like you took a mean son of a bitch like Blaze and turned him into a teddy bear," he says with a smile leaning back and crossing his arms over his chest.

Blaze stiffens beneath me, and I laugh, shaking my head. "The fact that you think I'm sweet also leads me to believe you are wrong about Blaze. I've been called many things in my life, but sweet was never one of them," I retort, rubbing Blaze's forearm around my stomach.

"Is that right," Hunter says with a raised brow.

"Don't get her started on name-calling. She'll have you all blushing with that mouth of hers," Bo speaks up, and I look at him, my mouth agape in surprise.

"My language isn't near as foul as yours," I spit back in mock shock. I hear the guys snickering around the table at our sibling behavior.

"Enough," Blaze says, getting our attention. "I call a meeting of the Outcasts to order. We have several new items that need to be discussed," he says firmly, and I lean back into him again, relaxing.

My eyes go to Bo and Mia, who are grinning at us getting to witness this. Everything I know about MC clubs, from the women at the underground fights, says that they don't allow anyone in church during a meeting except officers—especially not women. The thought makes my stomach tighten. That will not sit well with me.

"Before we start discussing the changes in Freedom and how it affects the club, I think we need Gia, Mia, and Bo to fill us in on specifics," Blaze says, and grunts of agreement follow around the table, as well as a few men pounding their fists on it.

My eyes go back to Bo and Mia. Bo gives me a small smile and a nod of encouragement. With a deep breath, I lean forward to begin.

"First, I want to know why Raphel is tied up in the basement and still breathing," Blaze says, digging his fingers into my hips.

I turn my face towards him as the rage I had felt earlier returns. "Because I found ledgers in his office proving not only kickbacks to the Mayor of Wells City but to others, along with information of him trafficking women. I intend to interrogate him before I send him to hell," I say with a raised brow.

"Do you want in on it?" I ask, meeting his gaze.

"Fuck yes," he replies, and I nod, turning back to the rest of the group.

"My dream of a new Freedom started a couple of years ago when I watched a video of someone complaining about ridiculous old laws still on the books in their state. It made me wonder what laws were still on our books. After some research, what I found surprised me," I say, looking at Mia with a grin and nod for her to take over.

She has been going through my notes and the law books. It's time she flaunts her intelligence a bit. Mia grins at me and then pulls her legal pad out for reference.

"Gia found some loopholes or laws that are still on the books that allow for a lot of leeway in how Freedom will be run," Mia says, flipping to the next page in her pad.

"For instance, did you know that Freedom was founded in 1925, well before Wells City was?" she asks, looking around the room. They all shake their heads, and she continues.

"A law effective in 1927 states that any individual or family owning 75 percent or more of a town or township have the right to set governing laws within said towns. The deed holder or holders of said towns can be deemed Mayor and govern as long as 51 percent of residents vote in agreement. However, section 5 b amends that stating that said towns must provide reasonable safety measures for said towns or townships to comply with the state by means of fire safety and a body of law to enforce and protect the town," she reads off then looks up making sure they are all paying attention.

"Go ahead, Mia," I encourage her.

She grins at me, then continues. "That's why a water tower is required because there aren't any fire hydrants in Freedom, but we will have to purchase a fire truck," she says, giving me a pointed look, and I nod in understanding.

"As far as a body of law enforcement, I'm assuming you have a plan for that?" Mia asks with a questioning look.

"Why not the Outcasts?" I say, looking around, and Blaze laughs behind me, making me turn in his lap.

"You want us to run Freedom?" He questions, with a surprised expression.

"Not just that. Freedom will be mine in a matter of hours: land, buildings, all of it. Mia will be the town planner tasked with its development and improvements," I say, pointing to Mia.

"Bo is my treasurer and running the main income source, fight nights and gambling," I point to Bo, who grins, sitting straighter.

Then I point to my chest. "I will be the mayor overseeing them. As a family, that leaves you and the Outcast with the rest. Setting and enforcing laws, ensuring the safety of residents, the fire department....Hell, there is a long list." I say, then look at Mia, who tears a sheet of paper out of her pad and slides it toward Blaze.

His eyes roam it as he works his jaw in deep thought. He lifts his gaze, looking around the room at his brothers, who are waiting not so patiently to hear what's on it.

"I'm just going to go down the list and read it along with the notes. Then you can pass it around, Blaze says, then clears his throat.

"Renovate Gym for Big C," Blaze's eyes flash to me with an appreciative look, and then he continues.

"Bar," his eyes twinkle, and he grins. "We have that covered."

"Grocery store, Clinic," he pauses, looking at Kane. "That's you if you want it," Blaze tells Kane, and he nods with a grin.

"Gas station," he pauses, looking at a man with Axel on his cut.

"You've been wanting to open a garage. The old gas station has two bays," he tells Axel.

Axel leans forward, placing his forearms on the table with a smile. "I'll do the work and run it if you're fronting the dough," Axel says, looking at me.

I return his smile, leaning forward to match his posture. "I'll do you one better," I said, looking around the room at all the Outcasts.

"You're family from this moment forward. Any member who wants to open a business in an existing building can do so, and I'll help them. With the agreement, 10 percent of your sales to cover upkeep and maintenance be paid into the town treasury monthly." As soon as the words leave my mouth, there are gasps around the room, followed by hoots.

"You mean you are willing to help us set up a business but only charge a 10 percent cut of gross revenue?" Hunter asks in surprise.

"That's right. I want Freedom to succeed. That means everything on that list has to happen and be successful," I say.

"All in favor," Blaze says in a raised voice to carry over everyone's chatter.

"Hooyah," is the unanimous response, followed by feet stomping.

"There is another matter I want to bring to the table before we go further," Blaze says low and deep. He leans forward, wrapping his arms securely around me, and several people get knowing smirks on their faces.

"I'm claiming Gia as my old lady," Blaze announces, and I immediately feel my cheeks flush as warmth fills my belly and my core tightens.

I knew this was how things work in MCs, but I never thought how it would make me feel when it happened. Being an Ol' Lady is the equivalent of getting married in the biker world.

Bo and Mia are smiling from ear to ear at my embarrassment. I look around the table as the excitement builds inside me. Resounding cheers and laughter fill the room.

I jerk slightly when Blaze's mouth nibbles on my ear lobe, and he growls. "You're mine now, Mi Alma. Are you ready to get burned?"

I squeeze my thighs together as heat floods my body, hearing those words. "Hell, yes, I'm ready," I say.

Suddenly, the bar doors swing open, and three prospects walk in. "Foods here," one announces.

I squeal in surprise as Blaze stands picking me up and putting me over his shoulder in a fireman's hold. He marches towards a stairway, chuckling. "I'm about to eat my breakfast," he shouts, and my nipples tighten at the realization he's talking about eating me.

Hoots and hollers are roaring out behind us.

"Don't break her the first time around."

"Remember, these walls aren't soundproofed."

Then I hear Bo yell out above everyone else. "Don't forget you still have errands to run today."

Shit, all thoughts of seeing the Mayor and my Nonno had left my mind with the excitement. They'll have to wait because my body wants Blaze. Hell, my heart wants to be connected to him in every way possible.

I cup his face in my hands, feeling the course stubble under my palms, and his eyes meet mine. The same desire I feel consuming me is blazing in his eyes. I need this man.

I run my hand higher over his head, feeling the prickle of his buzz cut as he turns the corner, pushing a door open with his shoulder.

Once we're inside, Blaze kicks it closed and carries me to the bed. He lays me down then climbs on top of me, his hard body pressing into my soft one.

Pushing his large calloused hands into my hair, his eyes searching mine.

"I'm a starving man, Gia. But I'm going to take my time with you." Then he captures my mouth in a heated kiss as he parts my thighs with his powerful one.

Chapter 15

Blaze

As I push my tongue into Gia's mouth, tasting the warm sweetness, the need to claim her is all-consuming. The desire to claim, taste, hell, to own her in every way is enough to drive a man mad.

I trail my lips and tongue down her neck, licking and sucking her supple skin as she throws her head back.

"Blaze," Gia moans my name, and my cock tries to jerk, but the teeth of my zipper are already biting into it uncomfortably.

I raise enough to grab the hem of her shirt, and she lifts, allowing me to slip it over her head. Throwing it to the side, I take in this gorgeous woman beneath me that is perfection.

My eyes slowly go from her toned stomach up to her full mounds spilling out of her bra, my hands following, needing to touch every part of her.

I cup a breast, then take a peak into my mouth, sucking it through the lace that is in my way, making me growl with frustration.

Gia thrusts her hips forward as she cries out my name again. I reach under her, flicking the clasp loose, then glide the offending straps over her shoulders and arms.

When her hard brown nipples come into view, I dive down like a starving man sucking, nibbling, and laving it with my tongue.

Gia writhes beneath me, grinding that sweet little pussy against me, reminding me it needs my attention. I rotate my hips, pushing my aching dick into her in response.

Forcing myself to release her breast, I sit back and trail my hands down to the waist of her pants and quickly undo them.

She lifts her hips, and I slide them off along with her panties. My control is slipping; I need to taste her. Lowering my body and pushing my broad shoulders between her thick thighs, I position myself for the first taste of heaven.

111

Inhaling her warm honey smell invades my nose, making my mouth water. Gia groans and runs her hands over my head.

Looking over her breasts, our eyes lock, and I dive in, licking from her opening to her labia, then her clit. When her unique taste hits my tongue, euphoria takes over.

What was once hunger is now an obsession, driving me to devour her.

Licking, sucking, flicking my tongue rhythmically as she jolts off the bed, cursing and gripping the sheets. I wrap my arms around her thighs, holding her tightly in place. Nothing will stop me now from eating my fill.

Thrusting my tongue inside that virgin hole that is now mine, she spasms around it, awakening the animal in me. A deep rumble erupts from my chest, and I make my way back to her clit, sucking it into my mouth while I slowly insert a finger into paradise.

I only get an inch or two in, and she is clamping down on it, trying to pull it further, and I oblige. Gradually easing my way further until I reach her barrier. I curl my fingertip up and find that perfect spot to send her soaring.

With increased suction on her clit while flicking it, I begin finger fucking her as her moans increasingly get louder.

Her hips begin thrusting in time with my finger, and her legs start to tremble.

Gia's whole body goes rigid as a scream of pure pleasure erupts from her full lips, and her pussy clamps down on my finger like a vise.

While licking and sucking, riding her through her orgasm, I pull my hand back, inserting a second finger knowing I need to stretch her. I'm not a small man, and as bad as I want to continue eating, my cock is demanding I claim her now.

Inserting two fingers to stretch her, I hungrily lick up all her cream, making her twitch and jerk.

"Fuck Blaze," she declares, making me grin as she grasps my head, trying to stop me.

Raising my head slightly, I grin, licking my lips. "I know you're sensitive, Mi Alma, but you'll soon learn when I'm hungry for this juicy body just to let me eat my fill."

Her eyes widen, but lust and passion are radiating off of her. She's now my addiction, and there is only one cure.

Standing from the bed, I remove my cut and lay it on the dresser. My eyes never leave hers as I remove my shirt, pants, and boots.

Gia's face shows surprise when I stand straight and reveal my rock-hard cock. I wrap my fist around it, running my thumb through the precum leaking from the tip, then squeezing it. Fuck I could nut just looking at her.

Climbing back onto the bed, hovering over her, I cup the back of her head, studying her worried face.

"You're big, Blaze. Bigger than I imagined," she whispers, but that spark of want is clear in her eyes.

I nudge her legs further apart, making room for me to settle my large frame.

I shift my hips, running my cock through her wetness. "You were made for me," I say, rocking back and forth, my stiff shaft stimulating her clit with each stroke.

"After I take your sweet cherry," I pause, thrusting over her aching little pearl again.

"I'm going to mold and stretch that wet little pussy so good it will never forget who owns it," I declare.

Gia's eyes flash, and she grips my shoulders tightly, digging her nails in. "Hell yes," she says.

I notch myself at her entrance while I stare into Gia's eyes. "I have been yours since we first locked eyes that night. Now you will be mine always," I declare with a ragged breath. I push forward, not stopping until I'm balls deep, bottoming out against her womb.

Gia groans, squeezing her eyes closed, no doubt at how I'm stretching her.

"Fuck! You're tight," I shout, using all my control to hold still while she adjusts to me.

Her walls are flexing, massaging me, making it nearly impossible not to move, so I grit my teeth. Her eyes open, and she loosens her death grip on my shoulders.

"My heart longed for you before I even knew you existed Blaze," she whispers, and my pulse races at her declaration.

"My soul recognized you the moment you entered the room. I knew then that there could never be anyone else, Mi Alma." I leaned forward and took Gia's lips with mine.

Holding her securely, I pull back with deliberate, controlled movements, plunging back into paradise.

Gia's legs wrap around my waist as I repeatedly impale her with my shaft. Gripping her hair, I tilt her head to the side to delve deeper into the kiss as my hips surge forward with new ferocity.

With every bump of her womb, she groans into my mouth, awakening a newfound need. Breed her, plant my seed, and watch her grow with my child.

Pushing up onto my knees, I hook my arms under her legs, lifting that sweet ass off the bed and making her call out.

"Blaze," she says, fisting the sheets.

I power my hips forward, slamming home, "Fuck Gia," I roar out. Every muscle in my body is alive and flexing as I take my woman. "Mine," echoes in my head as Gia holds on for the ride.

Sweat beads on my forehead as I watch Gia's chest rise and fall. Her breasts and face are flushed, her mouth open as sounds of her pleasure fill the room.

My balls begin to draw up, and jolts of my appending orgasm approaching shoot up my spine.

Reaching down, I begin circling her clit with my thumb.

"Yes, Blaze," she calls out, cupping her breasts and tweaking her nipples. The sight below me shoots me over the top.

Just as Gia screams out her release, I plant myself against her cervix as ribbons of cum leave me, filling her up.

I place my hand over her abdomen and look into her big brown eyes, staring back at me as our sweaty bodies twitch.

"We didn't use protection," she murmured, trying to catch her breath.

I shake my head. "I'm clean, you're clean. There will never be anything between us, Gia," I state with finality.

"I'm not on birth control," her eyes go wide, and I wrap her into my arms, rolling us to the side.

"I want everything with you, including a family," I say, running my hand down her back to that lush ass squeezing it.

"Putting my baby in your belly is my new mission," I grin.

She tilts her head back, looking up at me with surprise. "You want children so soon?"

I chuckle at her expression and then look lovingly down at her. "I want one for every year we're together until we're old and grey," I reply. She may think I'm joking, but I'm not.

Keeping my hands, mouth, and dick away from her is not an option. Just the thought of her swollen with my child has my cock rising for round two.

Feeling it pressing into her stomach, Gia's eyes widen, and I grin. "You get a reprieve for now because I know you're sore," I say, sitting up and scooping her into my arms.

Gia squeals in surprise. "Where are you taking me?"

"You're mine to protect, love, and care for now. A hot bath will soothe you while I clean you up," I tell her, walking us into the bathroom.

Once I sit her down to start the bath, I see her look at her thighs. The proof of her innocence is evident between them, and she visibly cringes.

"Hey, don't do that," I say, standing after the water is started. Taking her chin between my fingers, she looks up at me.

"You saved yourself for me, which is the greatest gift I've ever received. I'll cherish you always," I say, and then regret fills me.

"I'm so sorry I didn't do the same for you, Mi Alma. If I could go back and change things, I would," my throat tightens as I get the words out.

Gia reaches up, taking my face in her hands. "As long as you never touch another," she says, her eyes flashing a warning.

"Never," I say firmly. Not because I know she would cut my balls off if I did. It's the thought of touching any other woman makes me feel sick.

Gia nods her approval and steps into the tub.

I climb behind her while she does some weird knot thing with her hair, piling it up on her head. After she leans back on my chest with a content sigh, I soap the washcloth.

Starting at her neck, I caress and wash her as she lovingly traces patterns on my legs with her fingertips.

"Tell me something about you that no one knows," I say, washing her arms. I need to know everything about her, even her secrets.

Gia is quiet for several minutes, then sighs. "I hate my parents," she says matter of fact.

"I think most children feel that way at some point in their lives," I reply as I clean her.

Her hands stop moving, and she stiffens. "No, Blaze, I hate them. When I was a little, I would lay awake at night and pray they would die so I could go live with Nonno and Nonna," Gia's voice is barely above a whisper.

I wrap my arms around her completely, holding her to me. "Fuck Gia, what did they do to you?" I ask. I've always heard that her father was a mean son of a bitch, but if he hurt her, I'll end him myself.

"He never raised his hand to me, if that's what you're wondering. He has always been too afraid of Nonno for that. It was everything else," she said, resuming tracing my kneecap with her fingers.

I unclench my jaw before I crack a tooth. "Tell me," I demand, needing to know.

"The first time I knew what he honestly thought of me was when I was 10. It was late, and they were fighting as usual. I crept out of my room and knelt by the railing to listen," Gia's voice is sad, and my chest constricts thinking of her childhood being miserable.

"They were talking about the fact Mamma couldn't get pregnant after me and Papa called her worthless for producing a girl instead of a real heir. That was the first of many times it was made clear that not having a dick made me useless. I trained harder than his men, but it didn't matter. Eventually, his cruelty made me hate him," Gia's voice breaks, and I look down, tears streaming down her cheeks.

"Fuck Gia, I'm so sorry," I say, wiping her face, and my heart breaks for her that a father would say or do those things to his daughter. To make her feel worthless and unloved.

Gia sniffles and clears her throat. "That weekend, I went to Nonna's house, and we had one of our late-night talks in the kitchen over apples," she says with a chuckle, but I hear the longing in her voice.

"I told her what Anthony said," Gia's tone is cold and hard now.

"What did she say?" I ask, knowing from what I've heard that Nonna was a force to be reckoned with when she was alive.

Gia laughs. "She pointed to my chest and said that I have the North Star in me like her. To always listen to it and let it guide me. Not to worry about Anthony, to just be me."

I smile at that. "She sounds like an amazing woman," I say.

"She was. Anytime I need strength, I think of her words." Gia sits up and turns, taking the washcloth to add body wash.

Then she begins washing my neck and chest. Her hands and eyes on me have my dick rising out of the water. Fuck, this woman drives me crazy.

"Tell me something about you that no one knows," she says, throwing my words back at me as her eyes meet mine.

Now is the time to show her my demons. She deserves to see all of me.

"Over my career, I have seen and done many things I wish I could forget. But most of the time, I was proud to serve my country. The brotherhood with my unit I wouldn't trade for anything," I take a deep breath, watching her face as I prepare to tell her what I can about that awful day.

"Our last mission went sideways. It was supposed to be a simple rescue mission in and out before anyone was the wiser. Everything was going smoothly, and we were humping it into the enemy camp to retrieve our mark," I close my eyes tightly as those moments play in my head.

"Tommy was our youngest, always eager to charge into battle half-cocked. I ordered him to fall back with Hawk and Kane. Just as he turned around, we all heard the dreaded click and froze," I say, and Gia's eyebrows furrow.

"He stepped on an IUD," I state, and Gia's eyes widen in horror.

"Kane, Hunter, and I ordered him not to move and everyone else to get back. We circled, and I pulled my knife as we all knelt close. They are pressure-activated," I explain to Gia, and she nods in understanding.

"We tried digging around his foot to better look at it, but the sand is soft after a sandstorm. Both the IUD and his foot kept sinking further. We couldn't get to it to disarm it. It was a hopeless situation," I say, shaking my head, reliving that day.

"You don't have to tell me," Gia says, stroking my chest and neck as tears form in her eyes.

"I need to Gia. You need to understand," I say, and she nods, wrapping her arms around my neck and climbing onto my lap.

I hold her close as I continue.

"Once we all realized we were fucked Tommy shocked us all. He stood straight, not showing an ounce of fear. Telling us all he was ready and to move back away from him," I swallow hard, remembering the look in his eyes, knowing he was going to die.

"I ordered Kane and Hunter to move back. Of course, they argued, but we all slowly stepped away as his foot sank further into the sand. I knew it could blow any minute. Hunter was the closest to him and took off running at the last minute. He thought if he tackled the kid, he could shield him. It was too late for me to react as it happened," I say, barely choking the words out.

Gia searches my eyes for the outcome, but I'm sure she can guess.

"Hunter tackled him at a full run, and the IUD blew. It killed Tommy, anyway, blowing half his head off. Hunter was lucky and survived. It took three surgeries to repair the damage and remove all the shrapnel except from his spine. And there stood Kane, and I covered in their blood," I finish, not being able to describe all the aftermath and what we all had to do to get out of there alive.

Gia's eyes reflect the pain I feel inside. "I'm so sorry, Blaze. I can't imagine going through that. To watch as someone you cared about and depended on you die," she says, shaking her head, and I wipe the single tear that escaped running down her face away.

"We all deal with it in different ways. Hawk fights to work out his demons, and Kane sleepwalks sometimes now. Thor and Axel are trying to fuck their way through all female kind to forget the pain. I closed myself off to everyone until I met you—even my Pop. But you, Gia," I say, wrapping my hand around her delicate neck.

"You have filled the gaping hole that was in my chest and quieted my demons," I pull her to me, brushing my lips over her soft, full ones.

Chapter 16

Gia

After a few hours of much-needed rest, Blaze and I walk downstairs searching for food. His warm hand on the center of my back makes me grin as we enter the bar. We haven't stopped touching each other since he claimed me in church. I hope that never stops.

Mia sits at the table eating with the other guys, but I don't see Bo. We sit, and I rest my hand on Blaze's thigh as a prospect carries coffee over for us.

"Thanks," I say as he places the warm goodness before me. He nods and walks towards the back. Hopefully, it's the kitchen because I'm starving.

I look at Mia and ask, "Where's Bo?"

"There is a problem at the apartment, and he stayed behind until you woke up and could deal with it," Mia says, and I immediately stiffen.

"What's going on?" I ask, ready to leave if Pop or one of the kids needs me.

Mia sighs and sets her fork down. "It's the man. He is going nuts and calling for you. Well, for Mamma. He thinks you left him like Madre did. He bonded to you, Gia."

I feel my chest tighten at the thought of him in distress. Both he and Mia have had a rough life since her mother passed away. I pull my phone out and dial Bo. "Hey," he answers, agitated.

"How are you and the man?" I ask.

"He's calm now, but Gia, he's been pulling his feathers out and going crazy. I think you need to get back here and spend some time with him," Bo says, and Blaze squeezes my thigh.

I look up at him; he is close enough to hear us both. Blaze nods, letting me know we will be going.

"I'll be there in 30 minutes. Can you do something for me, though?"

"Sure, anything to get out of this apartment for a while," he replies.

"Take Mia and a few guys shopping for us. I'll give you a list; bring the bank bag," I say.

Bo chuckles, "Ya, you know I love to shop. See you in 30."

The line goes dead, and I slide it back into my pocket.

"What are we shopping for?" Mia asks as a prospect slides two plates of food in front of Blaze and me.

I take a bite and groan. After swallowing, I reach my hand out, motioning to her. "Give me your pen and paper. I'll make a list."

Mia slides them to me, and I start writing. Mia's wardrobe and essentials. 30x king beds, nightstands, dressers, linens, pillows, towels, washcloths, appliances for the kitchen, dining tables, couches, and big screen TV.

Blaze has been watching over my shoulder, and he lifts his head. "Has the Clubhouse been emptied?" he yells out.

"Yes, pres. Filled up one of those big roll-off dumpsters the contractor had delivered," one says, and my eyes widen.

Damn, I didn't think there was that much inside. Blaze laughs, looking down at my facial expression, and squeezes me.

I quickly finish eating with him and hug Mia, giving her the list. "Have fun on your shopping trip. Just have everything except your things delivered next Saturday to the Clubhouse," I say, using Blaze's words to describe our new home.

Mia smiles, and her expression softens. "Thank you, Gia. For everything."

I embrace her tightly and whisper, "You never have to thank me, we're family."

Pulling away, I look closely at her. "How are you feeling?"

"I'm ok, just sore," Mia replies. I give her a small smile hating that she has gone through what she has. Before

I go back to Blaze's side. I remember the mayor and the files.

"Do you have the files on the mayor with you?" I ask her.

Mia smirked and reached into her bag, pulling out a stack of folders and handing them to me.

"Thanks," I say, winking. Turning towards Blaze, he wraps his arm around my waist, guiding us out the door.

"We'll be at the apartment if anyone needs us," Blaze yells over his shoulder as we exit.

When we arrive at the apartment, I hurry inside as the first screeching sounds reach my ears. Blaze is right behind me, both of us coming to a halt in the living room.

Seeing the man on top of a curtain rod making awful noises and pulling at his feathers breaks my heart. Bo is beneath him, talking soothingly, trying to calm him.

I walk over and stand next to Bo with a sad smile. "Go help Mia and get some air. I'll take care of him."

Bo looks relieved and hugs me before picking up the bank bag and rushing out the door. I'm sure he is as stressed as the man is.

I look back up at this intelligent, beautiful bird and try to think how to calm him. Finally, I reach up and begin stroking a tail feather. "I'm here, baby boy. I didn't leave you; I just had things to take care of."

Hearing my voice, he raises his head and starts rocking back and forth. At least the loud noises stopped. "Bye Bye," the man says, bobbing his head.

"Yes, I went bye-bye but came home, didn't I?"

"No, bye-bye," he says, becoming agitated again, and Blaze pulls me closer.

"She has to work sometimes. But bye-bye isn't forever," Blaze tells the man.

He flaps his wings aggressively and jumps onto my shoulder, surprising both of us. I laugh, reaching up and running my fingertip over his head to his neck.

"Tickle, Tickle," the man says with a weird purr-like sound in the back of his throat.

Blaze chuckles at us and goes to the couch sitting. I follow while stroking the man.

"Do you like tickle, tickle?" I ask him.

"Tickle, Tickle," he repeats, pushing his head into my hand further.

"I think he has imprinted on you or transferred the mother connection he had with Mia's Madre over to you," Blaze says.

I nod in understanding. That makes perfect sense.

"We all need love," I whisper, looking at the man who has now climbed into my lap.

"Love Mamma," he says, making me smile. I've never had a pet before but feel connected to the man.

"Mamma loves the man," I say, and he begins bobbing his head like my words brought him happiness. He takes off to the corner perch that Bo set up for him.

It has toys hanging from the ceiling he can reach from his perch and his litter box below it.

"Is he trained?" Blaze asks with a confused look.

I laugh and shake my head. "I wouldn't have believed it if I hadn't seen it with my own eyes. But he uses the damn thing," I say, pointing to the litter box.

Blaze grabs me by the waist, pulling me onto his lap and kissing me gently. Our lips are in a tender dance. The connection I feel to Blaze as I wrap my arms around his neck speaks volumes without us speaking a single word.

He reaches up, cradling my face in his hands. It's a possessive hold as if he doesn't want me to pull away. I melt into his embrace, pulling him closer like it will merge our souls.

Our breaths mingle, and warmth spreads through me, intoxicating me. Blaze is not just tasting me; he is savoring every touch and lick with his mouth.

It sends a shiver down my spine, igniting a fire deep inside. Time stands still as we lose ourselves in each other. At this moment, there is only us, bound together by our connection.

Blaze tilts my head, deepening the kiss and plunging his tongue into my mouth. His slow, sensual strokes as he explores have my nipples hardening.

He tenderly strokes my sides but doesn't push further. His touch is intimate, conveying emotion, and I return in kind by running my hands over his neck and broad shoulders.

When we finally pull away, our eyes lock. Blaze's expression radiates love and promises of forever.

My pulse races as I run my hand around his neck and jawline. I never break eye contact as my hands cup his face. "I'm falling in love with you, Blaze. Hell, my heart is already there," I admit, staring into those big brown eyes that melt my panties with one look.

"Fuck Gia," he pulls my body to his chest, and our noses are almost touching. "I love you woman. Go ahead and fall; I got you."

I throw my arms back around his neck, slamming my lips on his. I never imagined I would have the ultimate partner who would love me unconditionally as Nonno and Nonna had. Sure, I hoped and fantasized. But doubt was always in the back of my mind.

To have the man of my dreams in my arms saying he loved me as I do him is overwhelming.

"Give me a kiss, give me a kiss," the man yells from across the room. We break apart, looking at him laughing. He seems happy now that we're here. But the reality is I have things to do today, and I can't just stay with him all the time.

Sighing, I lean into Blaze. "You're thinking of everything that needs doing?"

"Yes," I say, looking up at him. "I need to take care of this today. But I don't want him harming himself or getting upset again."

Blaze nods and gets a look of deep thought. "How do you feel about me having a few prospects come over to play and entertain him while we work?" he asks.

I sit up with a smile. "That would be amazing if it occupies him."

Blaze nods and pulls his phone out, sending a text. Once he gets a reply, he looks at me with a mischievous grin. "Hell, half the club was ready to head over. They love him," he says, and I burst with laughter.

It isn't long before the apartment is filled with Outcasts cracking jokes and entertaining the man. I grab the files, taking Blaze's hand as we go out the door.

"I feel like a parent sneaking away to work so their child won't cry," I murmur as we descend the stairs.

Blaze throws his head back, laughing, and then he looks down at me with heated eyes, making my stomach tighten. Shit, he is thinking about getting me pregnant again.

"Soon, Gia," his voice is low and sultry. I swallow hard, thinking of taking him back upstairs to the bedroom. But I can't; we need to take care of shit today.

"We need to go to the H.. Clubhouse," I corrected myself.

"Why?" Blaze asks as we reach his bike. I guess I'll be riding with him.

"I want to take the ledgers with us. Plus, there's a videotape I want to watch. I think Nonno still has a VHS player," I say, and Blaze nods.

I climb on behind him, holding tight with one arm and clutching the files with the other.

After we retrieve the ledgers and video from the safe, we leave for the mayor's office. During the entire ride, I contemplate my words. With all I know about the Mayor, I feel disgusted. He shouldn't be in office, but I remember something my Nonna once told Nonno. Sometimes, it's better to deal with a devil you know than to replace them with a devil you don't. You may end up with someone worse.

Blaze parks the bike outside of the city plaza, and we dismount. "How are you going to handle this?" he asks, taking my hand.

"By letting my bitch flag fly," I say, grinning at him and squaring my shoulders.

He smiles, and we march up the stairs and inside with determination. We never stop as we pass offices and go to the elevator leading to the city officials' floor.

When the bell chimes and the door opens, we confidently stroll out of it. I see a wooden door at the end with a desk outside.

Assuming that's the mayor's office, I march towards it. The woman behind the desk jumps to her feet. I've seen her before with the mayor at events. I guess I'm at the right place.

She tries to head me off, but I narrow my eyes and give her my don't fuck with me look.

"Miss D'Angelo, please let me announce you before you barge in," she pleads. So, she recognizes me. Maybe from one of my family's parties? I don't know and don't care.

"Step aside before I move you myself," I say coldly. Her face reddens, and she looks nervous, but she moves out of my way.

I step forward, open the door, and stride in with Blaze behind me. His hand is on my back, offering me support.

His stance and body language radiate power and dominance as we walk right to the far end of the room, where the chubby, balding little prick sits behind his desk.

"You can't just barge in here," he declares, hanging up the phone and quickly standing. When his eyes take us in, he stops staring at me with recognition, and I smile. It's not a kind one; it's an I'm gonna ruin your day smile.

"Sit down, Mr. Mayor," I say, enunciating every word. He slowly lowers himself into the chair, his gaze flickering from me to Blaze.

Then he looks at his secretary. "Leave us and shut the door," he bellows, and she does.

"What can I do for you, Miss D'Angelo?" he asks, folding his hands together on the desk, trying to look composed but failing miserably. His left eye is twitching, and by the movement of his suit jacket, I would say he is nervously bouncing his leg under the desk.

I slap the files on the edge of his desk with the video on top, then sit in a chair, crossing my legs. I hold his gaze without saying a word for several minutes while slowly tracing circles on top of the video.

The mayor visibly swallows hard and watches my movements. Does he know what's on the tape? Was Raphel blackmailing him? I need more answers, but first, I need to deal with getting Freedom signed over to me.

I pull his files from the stack, then the one from my research with the quitclaim deeds I had prepared. My eyes meet his, and I have to unclench my teeth, thinking of what is inside these files.

"You have 30 minutes to sign over all of Freedom to me. After that, you will cease to be involved in or with any drug dealers or human trafficking," I say, opening the files and ledgers so he can see the contents.

His eyes widen, and his hand shakes as he rubs nervously over his mouth and face. "It's not that simple," he says, his eyes still trying to look over everything I have on him.

So, I decide to make it simple. I start pulling papers and slamming them down. "Payouts, Kickbacks, women being trafficked for prostitution," with each word, I slam another piece of paper or photo. Finally, I pause, making a point to caress the videotape he keeps glancing at worriedly. Yes, there is definitely something important on it.

"Ok," he says, his voice sounding defeated.

I grab the stack of quitclaim deeds, putting them in front of him. "Get a notary in here now," I order, and his eyes widen.

"Now?" he asks like I would give him time to run or do something stupid.

Blaze walks around my chair and places his large palms on the desk, looking the mayor in the eye. "Right fucking now," his voice is low and deadly.

The mayor nearly jumps out of his seat. Then he grabs the phone, fumbling with it. "Suzie, get in here and bring your notary supplies," he says into the receiver.

Suzie, as I now know her, rushes in, looking around the room nervously. The mayor begins signing the deeds without reading them, and she starts notarizing them. I lean back, smiling.

When they are finished, he reaches them to me with shaky hands. "Is that all?" he asks with a squeaky voice, and I hear Blaze chuckle.

"You, your cousin, stay clear of Freedom. It's ours now," I say in a warning.

His eyes go wide at my knowledge of his crooked badge-wearing cousin.

"Never underestimate me or my family, for that matter, Mr. Mayor. Oh, and never address me as Miss D'Angelo again. I hate it," I say, gathering my things to go to the register of deeds to record these now making Freedom officially mine.

"What should I address you as then," he says, standing, trying to compose himself.

"Madam Mayor, or nothing at all. I don't like you," I spit back at him, turning and grabbing Blaze's hand as we walked out.

Blaze is smirking on the elevator ride down. "What are people supposed to address me as Madam Mayor?" he asks mockingly.

I raise my eyebrows at him as if he should already know. "Sheriff, Pres., Blaze, or the mayor's world. Any of those will be fine with me," I say, then smile slyly at him.

Blaze's eyes flash with heat just as the doors open. The look he gives me promises we will continue this later.

Chapter 17

Blaze

Riding through the gates to Mr. D'Angelo's estate, it's clear the rumors I've heard were understated. I see armed guards roaming the grounds and sprawling gardens on each side of the winding driveway.

When the mansion comes into view, it's not what I expected. It's grand but not cold like I imagined. A sprawling home that has been cared for comes to mind.

After I park, Gia and I walk inside hand in hand without knocking. An outsider would think she has lived here all her life.

"Nonno?" she calls out as we walk through the foyer past a grand staircase. An older woman with a warm smile comes out of the kitchen, wiping her hands on an apron.

"Gianna," the woman says, walking towards us with open arms. Gia stiffens slightly but smiles back at her, and they embrace. I've noticed she doesn't like being called that.

"Where's Nonno?" Gia asks, pulling away.

"He's in the study with Sammy. Who is this fine-looking man?" she asks, offering me a warm smile.

I can't help but return it. She has a motherly way about her. "I'm Blaze," I say with an outstretched hand.

"He's mine," Gia says with a twinkle in her eye, and the woman's face lights up like it's Christmas morning.

"Oh my," she says, clasping her hands. "You two go on into the study, and I'll finish making the cannoli," she says, spinning on her heel and walking away.

I chuckle, and Gia leads me through the house into a large wooden door. After she knocks twice, I hear a resounding "Come in."

We enter, and her Nonno is seated in an armchair with Sammy sitting across from him. They both appeared to be in deep conversation before we interrupted.

When Nonno sees us, he stands and opens his arms with a broad grin. "Piccola Ragazza." (Baby girl)

I release Gia as she walks into his embrace. "I missed you," she says, hugging him.

"Blaze," Nonno says with a tilt of his head, and I return it in respect.

"Sit, tell me how things are going," he gestures toward the couch.

Gia and I sit, her hand automatically going to my thigh. I place my hand over it, giving it a gentle squeeze. Nonno watches our actions closely with a smile.

I listen as Gia recaps all that has happened in the past few days up until now. Nonno's face goes expressionless, and his eyes are cold with the information.

He turns to Sammy, raising a single brow.

"Don't blame him for not informing you. I requested he let me tell you about Anthony," Gia says firmly.

Nonno looks back at Gia in surprise at her calling her Papa by name, but she ignores it.

"There is also a tape," she says, placing it on the coffee table.

Nonno picks it up and reads the label. "Insurance," he reads aloud.

"Do you have a VHS player so we can watch it?" Gia asks, and Nonno nods, walking to a wooden cabinet I hadn't noticed before opening the doors.

There is a TV inside with a VHS player on the shelf below. After he turns them both on, he inserts the tape, then takes a remote in his hand, stepping back.

We all stand, walking closer to watch.

A room of people sitting in chairs and some standing along the walls comes into view. The picture is grainy as I try to take everything in. A man at the front begins to speak loudly, and the chatter calms down.

"Tonight, we have a lovely selection of women up for auction," he pauses and gestures to his left. My stomach tightens at his words.

Men in suits begin pulling women out onto the stage. They are stumbling, trying to keep up, and they look off. They looked drugged. I hear Gia gasp and her Nonno curse, so I step closer, wrapping my arms around her.

Fuck I can't believe what I'm seeing. Are they just going to sell these women? Some can't be more than 18 or 19 years old.

As the auctioneer begins describing them and the bidding starts, I feel rage building inside me and tighten my hold on Gia to calm down some before I go hunting for them all.

"Nonno," Gia says in horror, pointing to the right corner of the screen, and my eyes follow.

Squinting them to make out the men in the back, I realize who she is pointing to. Anthony D'Angelo, her fucking Papa, and two of his men. He can't deny knowing where the money he was getting came from. The truth of everything is staring us in the face.

Gia begins to fall, and I catch her as her knees buckle entirely. She starts dry heaving, and I kneel beside her, holding her hair out of the way.

A small wastebasket is placed in front of her, and I look up to thank them, seeing Sammy. His jaw is set, and his eyes hold murderous intentions.

Before I can utter a word, curses leave Nonno as he steps closer to us, no doubt to assist Gia, but stops short, grabbing his arm, and a look of pain comes over his face.

"No," I yell, and Sammy springs into action, lunging for Nonno and helping him to the couch.

Gia pulls away to crawl to him, but that's not happening. Instead, I help her stand and go over to Nonno's side. She still tries to compose herself when she looks at Sammy and demands, "Get the doctor here now."

Sammy pulls his phone out and starts barking orders in Italian. When he puts it away, I see that Nonno's tie is undone, and his shirt unbuttoned. I feel helpless at this moment. All that I can think of is killing Anthony for what he has done to his Papa and daughter.

"I can't lose you, Nonno," Gia choked out, placing her palms on his chest.

He places a hand over one of hers and tries to smile. It comes out as more of a grimace. "I'm not going anywhere," he says lowly.

Gia nods, and I start rubbing small circles on her back to comfort her. It isn't long before several guards escort an older man with a black bag inside, taking Nonno upstairs to be examined.

To my surprise, Gia steps out of my embrace and walks to Sammy, standing toe to toe. Sammy's face, which showed worry moments ago, now goes serious.

"Blood in, blood out," Gia says in a dangerous tone I have never heard her use.

Sammy's eyes go wide. "You shouldn't know of such things," he mutters.

Gia lifts her chin in defiance. "Rule one," she says, demanding a response.

Sammy studies her face before answering. "Code of silence."

"Omerta," Gia responds, nodding. "Rule two," she demands.

Sammy stands taller and doesn't hesitate this time. "Code of honor, respect womanhood."

Gia gives an approving nod. "Rule three."

"Stay out of the drug trade. Violate these, and no man nor Madonna can save you," Sammy says firmly.

"That oath is taken by every made man and enforced by every Don. Break any, and death is the consequence. He has broken two. Don't make him issue the order on his own son," she says, her voice raising with each word as she points up the staircase where they took her Nonno.

Fuck is she ordering Sammy to carry out punishment? Sammy looks up at the staircase, and his jaw clenches and unclenches. Then he meets her eyes. Without saying a word, he pulls out his phone, barking orders, and then marches towards the door.

Gia turns, and I pull her to my chest. Lowering my head, I bury my nose in her hair, inhaling her. This woman is my world, but hers has to feel like it's falling apart.

Cupping the back of her head, we stand there like that in a tight embrace until the doctor descends the stairs with the guards. "He wants to see you," he says, looking from Gia to me.

"How is he?" Gia asks, turning in my arms.

"His blood pressure is elevated, but otherwise ok," he says.

"But the chest pain," she says with concern, lacing her words.

"Extreme stress can cause angina or anxiety attacks. Mr. D'Angelo has a history of them; that's why I suggested he retire before," the doctor sighs, then walks out of the room shaking his head.

I take Gia's hand, and her face shows relief that it wasn't more serious.

"Come on," she says, leading me up the staircase.

When we enter the bedroom at the end of the hall, her Nonno stands at the window staring out. His shirt and tie are neatly redone, and his hands are in his pockets like nothing happened.

When he turns towards us, I see pain in his eyes. This is a man that everyone in the city fears, yet right now, he looks almost broken.

Gia and I walk until we are a few feet away, and no one says anything for several minutes.

"Are you ok?" Gia breaks the silence.

"I am just dreading coming out of retirement," he says flatly.

Gia tilts her head to the side, really looking at him. "You have always had the perfect successor right under your nose."

Nonno's eyebrows draw together, and then a knowing look appears. "Sammy."

Gia nods. "For almost 20 years, he has been at your side faithfully. He's loyal, Italian, and holds your same beliefs. All you have to do is make him a made man," she grins.

I watch as Nonno considers her words. "He knows the family business better than any capo does," he says, speaking to no one in particular.

"Where is he?" Nonno asks, and Gia's whole body goes rigid.

"I sent him to deal with the problem. At the end of the day, Anthony is still your son, and no father should have to give that order," Gia says softly.

Pain flashes across Nonno's face, but his eyes show understanding. "Thank you," he says.

After a minute, he composes himself. Then he looks at me.

"I assume you claimed my granddaughter, as is your way?" he asks, and the question takes me off guard.

However, I don't hesitate to respond. "Yes, she is mine. My wife in the club's eyes." I say with finality.

The corners of his lips lift into a half-smirk. "Leave us piccola ragazzaa so we may speak," he orders, but Gia stiffens.

"I will not leave so you can talk about me behind my back," she says with defiance, and I chuckle.

"Fine," Nonno says, turning and going to a table, removing a small box from the drawer before returning. He opens it for me to see.

"I will not have my future grandchildren being born bastards. You married her according to your traditions; now do it according to ours," he says.

I look at the gorgeous diamond ring he is holding. I've never seen anything like it. A round diamond sits in the center of a halo of emeralds, and the setting looks antique.

"Nonno," Gia gasped. "You can't just demand that Blaze propose to me like that."

"I can, and I did. Besides, are you two already supposedly married to some extent?" he says with a raised brow.

Gia huffs then looks at the ring and covers her mouth. "That was Nonna's," she whispers.

"Yes, I gave her this on our first wedding anniversary. She would only wear it on special occasions, saying she didn't want anything taken away from her wedding rings. That won't be an issue for you if Blaze accepts it as your engagement ring," he says.

Hell, yes, I will. A family heirloom of her Nonna's. What man would turn that down? I accept the box and kneel, looking up at my woman. My future wife and mother of my children and take her hand.

Gia looks down at me, her cheeks flushed and tears pooling. "I love you, mi alma. Tell me you will be by my side always, bear my children, and be my wife." My heart pounds against my ribcage as I say each word. She is mine; I have claimed her. But making it legal is one more way to mark her as mine to the world. Then it hits me: I want my ink on her skin and hers on mine. Fuck, anything to do with Gia will never be enough.

"Yes," she breathes out, and I slide the ring on her finger, kissing it. I stand and pick her up, swinging her around, and she throws her head back, laughing.

When I stop, Nonno smiles, his eyes gleaming with happiness.

"We will have a drink to celebrate, then I want a closer look at those ledgers," he says, walking out of the room.

What the hell? I will never get used to how he and Gia can go from an emotional moment to all business in the blink of an eye. Today has been a roller coaster of shit, and his son is probably being buried somewhere right now. How the hell do they do it?

I feel hands gripping my face, and I look down, seeing Gia looking up at me. Her eyes search mine, which I'm sure shows my confusion.

"This is our way, Blaze. We don't dwell. We persevere and move forward," she says barely above a whisper. Then her face softens. "But if I need to fall apart later tonight or tomorrow, hold me?" she asks almost pleadingly.

Damn, this woman is so strong. I pull her to me, never breaking eye contact. "Always," I say, then kiss her.

Once we return to the study, Nonno sits in the same chair he was in earlier with a drink in one hand and a ledger in the other. "These entries marked D. Do you know who that is?" he asks.

I step away from Gia, walking over to look. As I scanned the page, I heard Gia answer him. "I'm not sure, but I'll find out when we interrogate Raphel."

Nonno looks up at her with a smirk. "I'm sure you will."

"I think the D is for the Diablo's. It makes perfect sense. They are rumored to traffic women and drugs. A few of my men have also spotted them close by a few times, but we haven't caught one yet to question them," I say.

"The Diablo MC?" Nonno says through clenched teeth, slamming his glass down on the table. I haven't seen him upset before, but the man is seething right now.

"Yes, I swore if I caught any of them in Freedom, I would bury them there, and I meant it," I state while fisting my hands at my side. They openly brag about their cruelty to their club women as well as trafficking others.

"We have a common enemy then," Nonno says firmly. "Let me know what you find out," he says, and I nod. Torturing information out of Raphel will be my pleasure after watching that fucking tape.

As if reading my mind, Nonno stands, removing it from the VCR and handing it to me. I take it but look at him, confused.

"Gia's instincts will be to burn it. My eyes are old, but they are still trained to look for details. Our mayor and a senator were in the audience," he pauses, watching my expression, which I'm sure is of surprise.

"Information and leverage are powerful things, Blaze. Collect them both to protect your family. Gia understands this," he says, shifting his gaze to her.

I look down at my woman, knowing there isn't anything I wouldn't do to protect her.

Chapter 18

Gia

I held on as Blaze downshifted, and we pulled into the parking lot of our new clubhouse. When he cut the engine, the sounds of construction work filled my ears.

We dismounted and walked hand in hand up the steps, passing a group of painters coating the exterior with a fresh coat of paint. Walking inside, we paused, looking at the flurry of activity by the workers.

Men carried out old carpets and appliances from inside while the sound of hammers and drills filled the air. We went through the chaos towards the back offices and spotted Sal writing on a clipboard.

"Hey, Sal," I said as we approached.

"Hello, Gia, Blaze," he greeted us warmly. "I'm glad you're here. My cousin is finishing up with the safe and needs you to choose a new combination," Sal said, turning and walking into the office to the right.

Blaze and I followed him in, seeing a shorter, younger version of Sal cleaning up some tools. When he noticed us, he straightened and grinned. "This must be Gia and Blaze," he said, stretching his hand and shaking Blaze's while I stood holding the files with Blaze's arm around me, looking at the safe.

He then turned and expertly lined up the dial while putting a weird-looking tool into the backside of the door. "You'll need to dial in the numbers you want while I drop the teeth from this side," he said over his shoulder.

I looked up at Blaze, thinking of the perfect numbers, and grinned. Walking over I turned the dial to my three numbers as he did his thing on the other side of the door. Those numbers meant the world to me.

Blaze looked at me questioningly, but I gave him a ask me later look and squeezed his waist. He winked, letting me know he understood.

Things are finally coming together and going according to plan. After putting the files and video into the safe and locking it, we walked back into the main lobby, or what will be our enormous living room and bar. Looking around, I took everything in, but my eyes stopped on the section of bare wall between the staircase and the elevator.

Cocking my head to the side, it hit me what needed to go there. I gently elbowed Blaze and pointed. "Wouldn't that be the perfect spot for a huge cage for the man? Like his own little house," I said with a smile.

Blaze studied the spot for a minute before asking. "What are you envisioning exactly because that bird hates cages now."

I walked over and stood in the spot but turned, facing Blaze and Sal, outstretching my arms.

"A 6 foot by 6 foot cage with an open doorway, meaning no door. He can come and go. But inside will be his perches, toys, and litter box. This would be his space or time-out area," I chuckled.

Blaze and Sal walked closer, looking at the spot like they were trying to picture it. "Sounds simple enough. We can do that," Sal says, writing on his clipboard. Anything else you can think of?" he asks, looking between Blaze and me.

I watch as a look of deep thought passes over Blaze's face, and he walks to a set of glass French doors that lead to the front porch. I walk to his side, wrapping my arm around him, waiting.

When he looks down at me with furrowed brows, I know whatever it is, it's important to him. "We need to fence the property for security," he says in a low tone.

I look outside and think of all the shit we've been through so far and what we could face with taking a source of income away from the Diablo's if they are behind the trafficking. Blaze is right. I turn, facing Sal.

"You heard him. We need a 20-foot fence and a gate entering the property," I say with a raised brow.

Sal begins retaking notes. "I can order the fence and gate installation once we finish the clubhouse remodel."

I nod because that will work out great.

"And I'll make sure the space is ready for your bird by the end of the week," he says.

I looked up, exchanging an excited look with Blaze. I could also see it in his eyes. This home, this town we are creating for our family, is finally all coming together.

After we're done, we ride back to my apartment.

Thoroughly exhausted from the day's stress, Blaze and I climbed the stairs to my apartment. "What were the numbers?" Blaze asked, leaving me confused for a minute.

Then I looked up at him with a grin. "The date of my last fight."

"To commemorate it?" he asked curiously.

"The night, yes, but not the fight. It was the first time I saw you," I say, feeling heat rise to my cheeks. But I will forever be grateful for that night.

"Fuck Gia," Blaze says before stopping mid-step and planting a kiss on me that has my toes curling. When he pulls back, his eyes are full of lust. "Later," he growls, then takes my hand.

Before we reached the top of the steps, the sound of fighting and the man yelling reached my ears. Blaze took the remaining steps two at a time, bursting through my apartment door with me behind him. What the hell is going on?

We both skidded to a stop in the living room. Bo and Mia are standing, mouths open with shock, much like mine, with their hands full of bags. They must have just gotten here, too.

The sight before me is shocking as I look around. The apartment looks trashed.

Prospects are standing around cheering amid overturned furniture and magazines on the floor. Hawk and Cowboy are sprawled in the center of the living room floor wrestling, all while the man is bouncing on his perch screeching at them to "Kick his ass."

I couldn't help it. Laughter erupted out of me. Were they doing this to entertain him, or is this normal for alpha males? The men in our family often fought in the gym to relieve stress.

At hearing me laugh, Blaze began chuckling at the scene before us. Once we calmed down, Blaze stood straight, his face firm.

"Stop! Clean this mess up," he ordered. His deep, baritone voice echoed off the walls, sending a shiver down my spine. Damn, everything about this man arouses me.

The room went quiet as Hawk and Cowboy broke apart. Mia and Bo turned to me with smiles, setting the bags down.

"Did you get everything you needed?" I asked Mia as she pulled me in for a hug.

"Yes, and thank you so much," she said.

"I told you to stop thanking me. Consider it a bonus for all the work you've been doing," I said, pulling away.

Mia's eyes went down to my hand, and she squealed. "Is that an engagement ring?" she asked, excitedly looking from Blaze to me.

Blaze wrapped his arm around my waist, pulling me back into his large frame. Everyone in the room froze, staring at us.

"Yes, we are officially engaged and making it legal this Saturday," Blaze announces to everyone with pride.

I lean my head back, looking at the love of my life. I've never felt this happy before. Wait, oh shit, how are we going to get everything ready in time?

"Blaze, I've never wanted some big fancy wedding; that's not me. But how are we going to put things together that fast?" I ask him worried.

"Look around you. We have help," he raises his head, looking around the room, and I do the same. He's right we can do this.

I jump slightly, making Blaze laugh at me when the Outcasts begin their usual loud hoots and hollers cheering. I guess I need to get used to it.

"Cowboy, can you see if your guy is free Saturday?" Blaze calls out, and he exchanges a look with Cowboy. My curiosity spikes when amusement flashes on Cowboy's face, and he nods.

I turn in Blaze's arms, putting my hands on my hips. "What's going on?" I ask.

"My ink on your skin, yours on mine, remember?" Blaze says, bringing my hand to his mouth and kissing it.

My whole body relaxes, and I melt. Damn, this man does things to me.

"What are we talking about exactly? Because he will ask," Cowboy says, walking up beside us.

I turn, grinning up at him. "We're getting matching wedding bands tattooed on our fingers. Nothing says commitment like permanent ink," I say with a mischievous smirk.

Cowboy's eyebrows shoot up into that black cowboy hat he always wears, but he smiles at Blaze." Damn, you are whipped."

"He's whipped, he's whipped," the man says, and we all laugh.

Cowboy jumps backward like Blaze will hit him. But to my surprise, Blaze chuckles. "Say what you want; you're just jealous."

A quick flash of pain crosses Cowboy's face, but it's gone as soon as it is there, and he side-eyes Mia. Then it hits me. He wants her, but why is he all growly towards her then? Why not talk to her or flirt?

Blaze cups my face, and my eyes go to him. With a silent shake of his head, I know he wants me to leave it alone. I lean into him and listen to the conversations around us.

Hawk is leaning against the wall next to Bo with his arms crossed. "So, what's your plan for the new warehouse?" I grin, remembering Blaze says Hawk loves to fight.

Bo grinned, puffing his chest out with pride. "Sunday through Thursday will be poker nights, and Friday and Saturday nights will be fight night. I'm gonna name it The Underground," Bo says.

I feel Blaze's chest vibrate beneath my cheek as he chuckles at them. But I feel proud not just of Bo coming up with an amazing plan to support the town but of us and our teamwork.

Bo turned toward Blaze and me with a mischievous glint in his eyes and picked up a bag off the floor.

"We stopped at AAA police and tactical supply on our way back," he said with a smirk, handing the bag to Blaze.

Blaze released me, opened it, and smiled. Dumping the contents on the dining table for us to all see. A pile of shiny star badges sat before us, and we all stepped closer as Blaze picked up the one that said Sheriff on it.

"One sheriff and the rest are deputies," Bo says proudly, laughing.

"I guess there's a new sheriff in town," Blaze lets out a deep, throaty chuckle, clipping the Sheriff's badge to his belt. Then he starts tossing the deputy badges to each of his brothers, the officers of the Outcasts. They catch them all smiling.

"Wait," Mia says, walking around the table, picking up her legal pad, and flipping through it. "I think there has to be a swearing-into-office ceremony by the mayor."

I grin at that, turning to face Blaze. "Angel Cruz, also known as Blaze, President of the Outcasts MC, do you hereby swear to protect the town of Freedom and all its residents under whatever damn laws you see fit to put in place to do so, and by any means necessary?" I ask loud and clear.

The snickering behind me makes it hard to keep a straight face.

Blaze reaches out, grabbing my waist and pulling me into his hard, muscular body.

"Fuck Ya, I do, madam mayor," he replies teasingly before crushing his lips to mine. The room erupts into cheers and whistles, but I ignore it, all too lost in the sensation of Blaze's lips on mine and the growing wetness between my thighs.

When I pull back, needing air, I know I can't ignore the fire in my core much longer.

All this teasing and touching has my panties soaked, and I need him.

"Umm, not to ruin the moment, but how are we doing sleeping arrangements?" Bo asks with a nod towards the man. Shit, I can't leave him.

"I can't leave the man, and Bo and Mia can't share a room," I say.

Cowboy growls lowly at my words, but Blaze smirks at him. He pulls out his keys from his pocket, removes one from the keyring, and hands it to Bo. "You can take my apartment until we move into the clubhouse," he tells Bo.

"Fuck yeah," Bo responds with a grin, already heading to his room to pack.

I look over at Mia and offer her a small smile. "You can stay in Bo's old room temporarily," I tell her.

Mia picks up her bags without acknowledging Cowboy's snarling as she passes by him.

I shake my head at how stupid alpha males can be sometimes. I turn to Blaze, my mind already on Raphael and the answers we need from him. "We need to deal with Raphael tonight," I blurt out.

Blaze's eyes darken, matching the anger on all of our faces. "Tonight, after the construction crew has left," he agrees, looking around the room at his brothers. "Meet at the clubhouse at 11 PM. We're going to end that piece of shit once and for all."

I tighten my hold on him as visions of torturing Raphel fill my head. We all know what a sorry piece of shit he is and the things he's done. I just hope there is a way to find the missing women.

Chapter 19

Gia

After everything calms down, the prospects leave for the night to switch shifts, patrolling Freedom, and Mia orders takeout for dinner for the rest of us.

Once the food arrives, the officers of the Outcasts, along with Mia, Bo, Blaze, and myself, eat while I listen to their playful banter as I watch our newly meshed family get to know one another better.

It's getting late now, and Mia decides to go to bed for the night. The Outcasts follow suit, leaving Blaze and me sitting at the table. He looks at me with a playful smile, then takes my hand, leading me down the hall towards the bathroom.

I watch with anticipation as Blaze shuts the door behind us and then turns to me. "Strip, Mi Alma," his voice laced with lust as he begins undressing, and my mouth waters as he removes his cut and t-shirt, revealing his toned, ripped abs.

I quickly undress while he adjusts the shower for us. Steam fills the room as we step into the spray of hot water. We begin caressing each other's bodies slowly, teasingly.

After several minutes of exploring each other, we take turns washing each other, and then Blaze turns me washing my hair. I can't remember ever having my hair washed other than at the hairdressers. The feeling of his firm, thick fingers massaging my scalp is otherworldly. My whole body goes lax against Blaze's hard one.

Once we rinse and dry off, we wrap ourselves in towels and walk to my bedroom. As soon as we're inside, I hear the door shut and locked, and then I am pushed up against the wall.

My breath hitched as Blaze's body pinned mine, his warm, callused hand sliding up my thigh, inching beneath my damp towel toward my core. A trail of fire followed in its wake, making my stomach tighten.

Blaze's lips hovered over mine, making my breathing ragged. "Every second, my hands aren't on you. I crave to feel your skin under my palms," Blaze says, sliding his fingers through my already wet folds, barely brushing over my clit.

"Blaze," I groan, leaning my head back against the wall, feeling a jolt of pleasure shoot through me.

He pulls his hand away, and I open my eyes to see him bring his fingers to his mouth, slowly sucking them clean. An animalistic groan rumbled from his chest, and his eyes locked on mine.

Blaze pulls them from his mouth with a pop. "I will never get enough of your delicious flavor, Gia," he says, spinning me around and stepping into me, forcing me backward.

I grip his shoulders as he walks us both further into the room. When I feel the bed hit the back of my legs, Blaze lowers me with his strong embrace.

"Now you're going to spread those sexy legs and give me what's mine," his voice is low and demanding, sending a shiver up my spine.

Blaze stands, dropping the towel from his waist to the floor, revealing his thick, long member that is pointing straight at me. He fists it, taking a long, hard stroke from root to tip and squeezing it hard.

I grab handfuls of the sheet below me and spread my legs. Blaze's eyes lower, and I know he can see how wet I am. His eyes flash, resembling a feral animal that finally catches its prey and is starving.

I lick my lips as my heartbeat roars in my ears with anticipation.

Blaze lowers to his knees and places my legs over his shoulders. His arms come around my thighs, locking me into place.

With his thumbs, Blaze gently parts my folds revealing my wet swollen clit. He inhales deeply, like he's savoring the scent of my desire, making my core clench. His breath ghosts over me, and I groan in frustration. It's torture when I'm waiting for him, but he takes his time.

"Mine," he growls. I grip the sheets tighter when Blaze's expert mouth dives in, sucking my clit into his mouth, all while flicking his tongue over and over, making my hips jolt off the bed with the intensity.

His fingers burry between my legs, probing and caressing my tight entrance while his other hand holds onto my thigh, no doubt steadying me for the storm he is about to unleash.

My breathing becomes more shallow and ragged. My nipples harden into peaks, begging for attention.

Blaze's gaze locks onto mine, and I see the feral hunger in them. He dives in, sucking my clit into his mouth. It drives me wild as the tension mounts in my core; waves of pleasure are building up, threatening to take me over.

With a growl, Blaze released my clit, running his tongue through my slit. His eyes glowed with a predatory look as he plunged two fingers deep inside me.

I gasped as he began stroking with deliberate, firm thrusts. His thumb begins flicking over my throbbing clit, sending my hips bucking to meet his movements. When he curved his fingers up, hitting that perfect spot inside, stars burst behind my eyes.

"Blaze," I yell, clutching the sheets tighter. The orgasm erupts from me, feeling too powerful. When my vision returns slightly, I see him grinning, and he quickens his pace.

"You're mine to pleasure, Gia. And pleasure you, I will," his voice thick with desire, sending a new wave of arousal through me just as I am coming down from the orgasm, he just gave me.

Blaze takes his other hand from my thigh and palms one of my breasts. Using his thumb and forefinger to pinch and roll my nipple, causing me to writhe beneath him.

In a swift movement, Blaze was on top of me. His face appeared almost frantic. Suddenly, his fingers were replaced with his thick shaft, and he thrust forward, filling me. The sudden fullness made me cry out with a mixture of pain and pleasure.

Blaze didn't give me time to adjust to him as he began thrusting in long, firm strokes. He was claiming me completely, utterly as our bodies embraced the carnal desire for each other.

I threw my arms tightly around his shoulders and my legs around his waist. Every thrust was forceful and controlled, leaving me trembling and gasping for air.

My walls clenched around him tighter as the pulses of pleasure racked through my body until the dam broke. My climax hit me so hard it felt like a tidal wave crashing over every inch of my body. An explosive burst blasted through me, and I cried out, burying my face in his neck. I am shattered.

I felt Blaze shudder above me, his hot breath ragged against my ear. He slammed forward one last time, planting himself firmly against my womb—the thick pulses of his warm release inside me.

Blaze buried his face in my hair, his panting slightly muffled. We stayed in a tight embrace for several minutes, allowing our bodies to come down from the high together.

Feeling his body weight on top of me is comforting—the warm pressure makes me feel safe and owned in this intimate moment.

Blaze's fingers began tracing small circles along my ribs, causing me to twitch with the tickling sensation.

"I love you, Gia," he whispered into my ear. His voice came out hoarse and raw, filled with emotion. He slowly raised his head, then leaned on an elbow, looking me in the eyes.

My breath caught at the intense look, and I softly cupped his cheeks, holding his face, and he caressed mine.

"I need you to understand that you're mine and only mine, Gia," he said. His tone was low and commanding, and I felt warmth fill my chest. This man is everything to me.

I clasp my arms tight around him, pulling him as close as possible. "And you're mine, Blaze, only mine."

Blaze began kissing my face all over before pressing his lips to mine. It was soft and passionate. We were sharing a promise of both fidelity and unconditional love at this moment. I felt it, and I know he did, too.

When we broke away, Blaze flipped us so that I was splayed across him, his manhood still firmly inside me.

"We will sleep like this tonight and every night until my seed takes hold," he said, rubbing his large hand up and down my back while his other cupped the back of my head, holding it to him.

We lay there wrapped in each other's arms, silence filling the room, and it was comforting. I could feel his breathing evening out, and I began to feel myself drift. This is how I want to fall asleep every night, was my last thought before falling asleep.

The ringing of Blaze's phone jolts us awake. He answers it with a gruff "What?"

I can hear Cowboy's deep voice on the other end telling him it's 10 pm and not to forget about interrogating Raphel. Blaze looked down at me, still splayed on top of him and tangled in the sheets.

I rise, sitting straddling him, and nod. I then slid off his now-soft shaft standing. I quickly grab a towel off the floor, wrapping it around myself to clean up in the bathroom.

After cleaning up, I return to my room to get dressed. I pulled a pair of black jeans and an old band t-shirt from my closet when Blaze's voice startled me. "No panties or bra, Gia?" He asked with a raised brow from across the room.

"I'm in a hurry," I replied, feeling flustered.

Blaze came over and embraced me in one arm, his other hand cupping my breast beneath the baggy t-shirt. "Don't make a habit of it," he warned in a possessive tone. "I can't stand the thought of anyone seeing what's mine."

I let out a groan as he gently squeezed my breast, and I muttered, "OK."

We left the apartment, each of us straddling our motorcycles and starting the engines. The cool night air whipped through my hair as we headed to the new clubhouse.

Thoughts of how we were going to torture the information we needed out of Raphel ran through my head. His illegal brothel, the kickbacks he was paying to the mayor, and who is 'D'? This 'D' person or group was out there auctioning off women in a trafficking ring, and we need to stop them and hopefully help the women.

As we pulled into the parking lot of our soon-to-be clubhouse, I felt a wave of excitement wash over me. I've seen many interrogations before growing up but never ran one.

Conjuring the images from that videotape, a calmness flowed over me along with rage. They are a strong mixture. I know I won't have any trouble hurting or killing Raphel.

Blaze took my hand, and we made our way inside. It's dark with only a few dim lights turned on by, I assume, Cowboy or one of the Outcasts.

We find Bo and Cowboy standing at the top of the basement steps, waiting for us. They both gave us a slight nod before we all descended the stairs, none of us speaking.

Once we reach the bottom, I see Raphel is still hog-tied, lying on the cold basement floor. I squint at the harsh fluorescent lighting that is too bright for my tired eyes.

In one corner, I spot a table covered in various tools, no doubt from upstairs. Hammers, drills, a crowbar, and various other things have my hands itching to bring pain to Raphel for what he's done. But we need answers first.

Raphel's pathetic pleading filled my ears as Hawk and Kane grabbed him, standing him up. Then Blaze removed a pocket knife and began cutting the ropes free.

"Who tied him like this?" Cowboy said, laughing, shaking his head no doubt at all the knots I placed at various places.

"I did," I replied with a smirk, meeting his eyes.

Bo came to stand next to me, wrapping an arm around my shoulder with a look of pride on his face. "We used to practice tying each other up and escaping as teenagers," he says with a shrug, and the room bursts into laughter.

Then it hit my nose. The smell of piss and shit made me gag as they brought Raphel to the center of the room, dropping him. Damn, he smells rank.

I stood back with Bo, watching Blaze order them to stand him up. The other officers of the Outcasts gathered around to witness this. They didn't know everything that Blaze and I did, only parts.

Between each punch Blaze threw at him, he asked Raphel a question. If Raphel hesitated or wasn't truthful, Blaze would rein down blows until he got the answers.

'D' was, in fact, an abbreviation for the Diablo's. They had found out about Jose and Raphel taking over Freedom and their little enterprise and stepped in.

Jose and Raphel were too happy to give them a cut for additional protection and provide the Diablos with young women. Women they kidnapped off the streets or from bars in surrounding cities to be auctioned off for a 25 percent cut.

The whole thing makes me sick. Treating women, no better than cattle to be turned into slaves? Whores? I can't even wrap my head around what all these women have been going through.

Raphel set up a hidden camera at one of the auctions once he saw that influential people were attending to buy women. He got money hungry. Except somehow it backfired with the mayor.

I can't stand here any longer. We've got the information we need. I pull away from Bo, and my body vibrates, wanting to unleash pain on Raphel and end him in the name of every woman who has been hurt because of his actions.

I grab Blaze by his bulging bicep, and he turns, looking down at me. I'm sure he can see my rage and the unshed tears in my eyes. Not because I feel like crying, it's because my body doesn't know what to do with this much anger.

Blaze gets a knowing look and kisses my forehead before stepping back.

"Release him," I order Kane and Cowboy as I walk over to the table of tools, running my fingertips across them. I stop when the cold metal of the crowbar sinks into my skin, and I smile.

Grasping it firmly, I turn, looking down at the sniffling, pathetic man balled up on the floor, begging for his life.

I look up to Bo, my best friend, who has always been at my side when we have dealt out justice in the past for the kids. He meets my eyes and nods, walking over to the table and picking up the hammer.

I look back at Raphel as he tries to get up on his knees. "Did the women beg you to stop or let them go?" I say in a deadly tone.

"Yes," he squeaks out, trying to crawl away.

I cast the crowbar over my shoulder and unleash it forward, striking Raphel across the back. A resounding crack fills the room as he screams out in pain, dropping to his stomach.

Bo walks around, standing at his head. "Did they beg not to be drugged or touched?"

"Yes," Raphel barely chokes out before Bo stomps on his wrist and then brings the hammer down on his hand.

"Please just kill me," Raphel pleads through his cries of pain.

"Do you think those women you men sold off have begged for that same thing as they were raped or tortured by whoever bought them?" I ask, venom lacing every word as I raise the crowbar again, aiming it at his head.

Raphel's eyes seemed to come into focus as they met mine. "Yes," he whispered lowly, almost as though that thought had never entered his mind.

"Fuck you and the Diablos," I yell as I bring the crowbar down with all my strength, splitting his head open. I try to pull it back to keep going to unleash the fury inside me, but it is lodged firmly in his skull.

I scream into the room until I feel warm, strong arms wrapping around me. I know instantly that it's Blaze—my amazing man. I release the end of the crowbar, melt into him, and let the tears fall.

Bo looks at me, and his eyes match how I feel—sadness for the women, rage for what has been done and is possibly still happening to them.

Kane steps beside Bo, handing him a military knife from the sheath on his waist. Bo thanks him and kneels next to Raphel, whose body is jerking and twitching. "You got off easy in my book, you son of a bitch," Bo says, then slices his throat, putting an end to him.

I turn in Blaze's arms, my fists clutching the back of his shirt. He cups my head as his chest rumbles with his next words. "We'll get the Diablos, I promise—every last one. Then we'll try to find the women and get them help."

I nod in agreement and take a deep, calming breath.

"Get him out of here and clean this up. I need to get Gia home," Blaze says, then picks me up bridal style, carrying me towards the stairs.

I hear the men talking behind us. "Damn, he picked the perfect woman to stand by him," one said.

"Now we know why she wants a crematorium. It will come in handy," another voice rumbles.

"Remind me not to piss her off," Cowboy said. I recognized his voice and buried my face into Blaze's chest as he climbed the steps.

Chapter 20

Blaze

After I reach the parking lot, I lower Gia onto her bike. She looks up at me with those big brown eyes with concern.

"I've never killed a man before," she confessed. "I've hurt them and watched interrogations where men were killed. But this is the first time I've taken a life. I've never wanted to hurt someone so badly as I did him."

My chest constricts at her words. How do I explain to her the strength I see in her? How her big, protective heart make me love her more?

"First, you technically didn't take his life. Secondly, I think you're a force to be reckoned with," I tell her firmly, cupping her face. "A strong woman who fights for what she believes in. It makes me love you more, Gia, my Rebel." And with that, I lean down, kissing her passionately.

When I pull back, I can't help but grin. "I'm now loving the idea of a crematorium."

"Me too," Gia replies. Besides, it can also be helpful to the family," she says, and now I'm curious.

"What do you mean?" I ask.

Gia explains that it's customary for the bride and groom to receive a gift from the family in the Mafia. But also, from them to the Don as a show of respect.

"I was thinking our gift to the Don could be our disposal services," Gia says with a smirk. "They would have to drop off to us, of course," she says calmly.

Fuck she's serious. I guess it makes sense. I'm marrying a Mafia princess. She may hate that title and what it stands for, but that doesn't change facts. I kiss her again before straddling my bike. We need to get back and sleep.

This entire week has flown by in a flurry of preparations for our wedding. As soon as Gia called her Nonno, he took charge of planning and arranged for a large white party tent to be set up in the backyard of the new clubhouse for the ceremony.

Nonno was adamant that decorations would adorn the tables, an open bar would be fully stocked, and catering and music would be organized.

He also asks Gia if he could have the honor of walking her down the aisle, and she has been floating on cloud nine ever since. They are more like father and daughter every day, and I love seeing how it makes her so happy.

Nonno came out of retirement long enough to make Sammy a made man. Now Sammy has taken over as Don of the family, allowing Nonno to rest easy in retirement again. I'm thankful because Gia has worried about his health since the day, he had chest pains.

It's Friday, and Gia and I are sitting on the couch talking with Bo and Mia when Gia's phone rings. "Hello," she answers. I lean closer so I can hear.

"Hey, Gia. We've finished the renovations on the clubhouse if you and Blaze want to come by and take a look," I hear Sal say, and Gia's face lights up, looking at me.

I grin and nod as I pull my phone from my pocket, texting Cowboy so he can let the guys know. They will all want to see our new home too.

Once she hangs up, we fill Bo and Mia in on what's happening and head to the clubhouse. When we pull in, the entire Outcast MC, including prospects, are waiting except for a few on patrol.

Sal is standing proudly on the porch, waiting for us. He showed us around the entire downstairs while pointing out each detail of the renovations. Gia and I were both impressed with the work they had done.

He stops in the center of the hallway to the offices, making us all stop. "Do you trust everyone here?" Sal asks, looking from Gia to me.

"Yes," we reply in unison, and I wrap my arm around her waist. My brothers all stepped closer, intrigued by the smile on Sal's face.

"As you can see throughout the old Grand Hotel, ornamental panels are on the walls. We used that as our inspiration for hiding the basement entry," he says, pointing.

"But we improvised with the trigger mechanism," Sal says, pointing to the little round wooden buttons in the hallway but not in the other rooms around the wood molding.

"Push the 6th one in from the floor," he says.

I reach up with my free hand and push the wooden button that he said, and I hear a click, and the panel opens a mere inch towards me.

"Shit," Gia murmurs at my side, making me laugh.

I look at Sal with amazement. "This is clever as hell," I tell him.

"I know," he says cockily with a chuckle. "All you have to do is push it closed to lock it again. There is also a release inside to get out if you're ever shut in," he grins.

After we finished looking around and my brothers announced they were going upstairs to pick their rooms, Gia stiffened beside me.

I looked down, seeing a look of deep thought on her face. "Hang on a minute," she said, and they all stopped mid-step, turning towards us.

"I'm going to ask two things of you guys, and you may not like them," she says firmly, and I hear a few curses making me stiffen.

"You will show her the same respect you show me. Understood?" I order. None of my brothers utter a word and wait.

"First, I want to say I know how many MCs operate from women I have met at fights. This is my home, your home. I don't want club girls or your pump and dumps here. I don't want to worry every time I sit down somewhere if I'm sitting in one of your cum stains," she says, and I can't hold back my laughter.

I understand where she is coming from, and they need to also. We plan on raising a family, and I don't want my kids seeing that shit. I look around the room, and several of my brothers are scowling and muttering under their breath.

"Are you saying you don't want any woman here except you and Mia?" Axel asks, and Thor agrees with his question, stepping up beside him. Of course, these two would complain.

"No, I'm saying if you're not interested in a woman being your old lady or at least want to get to know her better, then screw her somewhere else. Don't bring her here." They nod, but I see the disapproval on their faces.

"What's the second thing we won't like?" I ask Gia, looking down at her.

She takes a deep breath and turns, facing me, squaring her shoulders like she is preparing me to argue. I don't like this already.

"I may own this town on paper, but we are getting married. Not once have I mentioned a prenup, and I won't. I want us to be equal partners in everything, Blaze. That means I won't be shut out of the club like other MCs do to their women. All of you are equals in running Freedom. Actually, I would prefer to handle development and administration while you guys handle the day-to-day and law enforcement. I want a place at the table in church at your side just like I think all your women when you find them, should have one," Gia says, turning towards my brothers and eyeing them.

I'm frozen in my spot. I hadn't thought of this, nor had we discussed it as a club with everything going on. I look around at all my officers and prospects standing, staring at Gia like she has three heads.

I flex my jaw as I think about her words. We are partners, and I want that in every way. "Gia has given us more than just our club to run. She has given us a town, businesses, and more control over our lives and future than we ever imagined. Keep that in mind before each of you vote. Yay or Nay?" I state in a loud, clear voice.

I may be the president, but we vote on matters affecting the club. Many of my brothers appear to be thinking, but Cowboy and Hawk immediately step toward us.

"I, for one, don't think it's too much to ask. You say you're going to consider our opinions and thoughts when it comes to the town. Hell, even helping us open businesses," Hawk says, then looks at me. "I vote yes. She sits at the table and gets to voice an opinion on matters if she has one."

Hawk steps back, and Cowboy stands straighter. "I vote yes."

I smile and watch Hunter, Kane, Axel, and Thor finally vote yes.

I take Gia by the hips, pull her towards me, and kiss her head. She looks up at me with a smile, then looks back at our family.

"Pick any room you want. Just leave Blaze and me one on the first floor, please," she announces with a grin.

"My room is beside theirs," Mia yells, taking off after the guys. Even Hunter rolls into the elevator to take a look at the rooms.

"Have you seen them yet?" I ask Gia. She turns in my arms, shaking her head.

"I was only up there when we came to take out Raphel and his men. But from what I remember, they are all the same—large open spaces for the bedrooms with high ceilings and ensuite bathrooms. Only one window in each room, though, except for the French doors in each room that leads to the balcony," she says with her head tilted to the side.

"Every room has a door leading out to the balcony?" I ask, amazed.

"Yes, front and back of the clubhouse. There are five rooms on the front and five on the back for each floor," she grins.

"30 rooms," I mutter. That's plenty for everyone. I look at the elevator, thinking how great that is for Hunter. He always had a hard time anywhere he goes with the wheelchair. Gia has made this a home for all of us.

"Thank you for the ramp and making sure the elevator was operational. The way you thought of us all in your plans is," I pause, trying to find the words.

Gia reaches up, cupping my face. "Don't thank me, this is our family."

I nod but grip her hips tighter. Fuck, this woman amazes me.

A loud throat clearing behind me gets my attention, and I turn to see Sal leaning against the wall with a grin. Fuck I completely forgot about him.

"We'll be back on Monday to begin fencing the property for you," Sal says, reaching out his hand for me to shake.

After he walks out, Gia takes my hand and leads me to the office at the end of the hall. It has a large wooden desk to the right with bookshelves behind it. I scan the room, and the entire left side is empty.

"Is this going to be your office?" I ask. This is by far the biggest of them, even larger with the one next door to it with the safe in it.

"No," she replies, and I look down at her, seeing a mischievous grin. "I was thinking this is perfect for you. It is large enough to put a big enough table and chairs in to hold church."

I look around again with new eyes. She's right. This would work great. It's large enough for everyone, including women, if my band of brothers find theirs. We just need to get a table built.

As if reading my thoughts, Gia wraps her arms around my waist and lays her head on my chest. "We'll get everything figured out," she says.

We hear a loud noise and turn towards the door, following the arguing through the empty clubhouse into the kitchen. Two prospects are bickering like old women when we step through the doorway.

"What the fuck is going on?" I ask. They look at each other, then look at me but say nothing.

"Spit it out," I order.

"We were discussing where things should go," the older of two says, and Gia starts chuckling beside me. The sound is music to my ears.

160

"Aren't you two the ones cooking at the bar?" Gia asks them with curiosity.

They both nod with smiles.

"Do you cook?" one prospect asks.

But I hear Bo's voice from behind us before Gia can answer.

"Don't ask her to fix you anything besides basic breakfast food. She will either burn it or poison you," he says with a smirk.

Gia spins around, pointing her finger at him. "It was only once, and I swear you had the stomach flu or something because I was fine after eating it."

"If that's true, why did I feel fine 2 hours later?" Bo asks with a raised eyebrow, and Gia huffs, turning back towards the prospects.

"No, I don't like to cook. If you two want the kitchen to be your domain, have at it," she smiles, waving her hand around.

The two prospects immediately start discussing what foods need to be stocked in the pantry and where plates and glasses will go. I shake my head at them. Shit, you would think she told them tomorrow was Christmas.

Chapter 21

• • • •

Gia

Loud ringing jerks me awake. With a groan, I fumble to find my phone on the nightstand. Shit, it's barely daylight. Who's calling?

"Hello," I answer.

"Good morning, Gianna. Are you awake?" I hear Nonno's voice come over the line. Blaze rumbles beside me.

"I am now," I say groggily.

"I wanted to see if you needed anything before the wedding. It's only 4 hours away," Nonno says.

"Yes, I think so," I reply, resting my head on Blaze's chest.

"Did you and Mia find dresses you liked?" Nonno asks.

"No, so I'm going to get married in my jeans like Blaze," I say.

"What! No, you're not. You are a D'Angelo and a princess at that. I'll have a stylist there in an hour with a selection for you and Mia to choose from," Nonno's voice is firm.

"Who is that, Gia?" Blaze asks, and I look up at him.

"Tell me you didn't break tradition? Is that Blaze I hear?" Nonno asked, shocked.

"Yes, Nonno, it's Blaze. It is modern times, you know," I retort. "Well, his Pop and I are on our way. He better be dressed when we get there," Nonno says, and then the line goes dead.

I wrinkle my nose at the phone before returning it to the nightstand. Blaze's eyes flutter open, a full-bodied yawn spreading across his lips. He looks at me through half-lidded lids before a slow grin crawls across his face.

"Seems like you're in hot water," he murmurs, wrapping an arm around my waist and pulling me flush against him. The rough warmth of his skin against mine sends a shiver down my spine.

162

"Shut up, Blaze," I say, burying my face into the crook of his neck. He gives a hearty chuckle, the vibrations traveling straight to my core.

"Nonno and your Pop will be here soon," I tell him.

"At first, I liked those two hanging out. Now, I'm not so sure," he says.

Blaze's hand slips lower, and his fingers find the naked curve of my hip, sending a jolt of electricity through me. His touch ignites the primal urge within me. The sensation overpowers the annoyance of an early morning phone call, shifting my focus to his sensual teasing.

"Who do you belong to, Gia?" His voice is husky, rough with sleep and desire.

"You," I murmur against his chest, feeling the vibrations of his laugh rumbling beneath my cheek.

"And who do I belong to?" His fingers trail up my spine, and I shiver.

"Me," I sigh and press even closer to him.

He captures my lips with his own, drowning everything out with a passionate kiss that leaves us both breathless. Our bodies rub against each other as his hands roam, making my nipples tighten.

The moment is interrupted by a knock on our bedroom door, followed by a voice - "Gia, the stylist is here." Mia yells.

I pull away reluctantly, murmuring against Blaze's lips, "Duty calls."

"I'll be at the end of the aisle waiting for you," he replies with a smirk.

Blaze stretches each of his muscles, rippling along his torso, making my mouth water.

"For the record," he says, walking to the closet.

"I like your jeans idea. Your ass looks great in them," Blaze chuckles.

"Really?" I muse, walking over and locking eyes with him as my fingers wander down his muscular chest, grazing over his hardened abs that flex at my touch.

It's time I did some teasing of my own. "I want something from you tonight," I say, grinning.

A playful growl resonates within him as he spins us, pinning me to the wall in one effortless move.

"What's that?" Blaze asks, running his nose up my cheek.

"To taste you," I say between ragged breaths.

"Gia," he murmurs between kisses that trail along the shell of my ear down to the base of my throat. I arch into him — an involuntary response to his electrifying touch — reveling in the rough stubble grazing against my skin. Every stroke of his tongue sends tingling waves down to pool deep within me.

"Gia," Mia yells, breaking us out of our moment. We pull away, and Blaze slaps my ass.

"Go on. I'll be out in a minute," he says.

I quickly put on a T-shirt and a pair of shorts, walking into the living room. A woman in her 30s with long blonde hair and makeup done to perfection is neatly arranging dresses on a rack. I look over at Mia, who is by another rack of dresses looking through them.

"Nice tits," the man says, making me spin around looking at him. He is bouncing on his perch, looking at the stylist.

I'm sure my mouth is hanging open in shock. The woman laughs and walks over to him. "What's your name?"

"I'm the man," he replies, making her giggle like a schoolgirl.

"I'm Rachel, the man. Nice to meet you."

"Nice tits," the man repeats, and I rub my hand down my face, but I can't help but smile at the little shit. He's funny.

"I'm sorry about him. He's been spending time with the guys lately, and I think they've been teaching him things they shouldn't," I tell Rachel, trying my best to sound apologetic.

"Don't worry about it. It's the best compliment I've had today," she smiles.

Seriously? Does she consider that a compliment? I shake my head and look back at the rack of dresses Mia is going through.

They are colorful, resembling cocktail or formal dresses that catch my attention. I've never pictured myself wearing a poofy white wedding dress. Maybe I'll like one of these.

I hear the bedroom door open, and I turn to see Blaze. My eyes roam him from head to toe. He's wearing a tight black pair of jeans that hug his thick thighs and ass perfectly and a black button-down shirt with his cut.

I try to be discreet as I rub my thighs together, and our eyes lock, and he smirks at me. Actually smirks.

I grin, slowly cupping my breast through my shirt, and his eyes follow the movement. His jaw clenches, and then, in three long strides, he is in front of me, grasping the back of my head with one hand while the other pulls me to him by my waist.

"You're playing with fire again, Rebel," he says low and deep. The rumble of his chest has my stomach tightening.

"And you're starting something you can't finish," I retort just as there is a knock at the door.

I straighten myself while Mia answers it. Nonno and Pop walk in, looking around the room, and then head straight for Blaze and me.

"You shouldn't have stayed here last night. Hell, you shouldn't be here now. It's bad luck," Pop says, pointing a finger at Blaze, and I laugh.

Nonno looks at me with a disapproving look. I know he is old-fashioned in many ways, but he needs to get with the times.

I put my hands on my hips and meet his stare. "Do you buy a car without test-driving it?" I ask him.

Nonno's eyebrows scrunch together, confused. "No."

"Well, neither do I," I grin, and his eyebrows shoot up into his hairline. To my surprise, he throws his head back and lets out a deep belly laugh.

Mia steps beside me and elbows me, getting my attention. She has a deep scowl when I look at her, but she isn't looking at me. I follow her line of sight and see Rachel licking her lips and checking Blaze out like she wants to eat him up.

Nonno, Pop, and Blaze stop laughing and turn to see what I do. Rachel is now running her fingers between her breasts like she is getting aroused. Oh, hell no!

I push past Blaze, wrap my hand around her throat, and slam her against the wall. Rachel's eyes widened, and she grabbed my arm with both hands as if she could pull me off. Not a chance I'm pissed.

"Get off me," she chokes out.

"Mamma's pissed, Ut Oh," the man yells.

Rachel turns slightly and says, "Oh, shut up."

Now I'm seething. I lean, so my face is mere inches from hers. "You come into my home, disrespect me by eye fucking my fiancé right in front of me and my family, then you have the nerve to speak to my bird like that?" I pull her forward and then slam her head back into the wall.

"Aah," she screeches in pain. I grab her by the hair and arm, marching her to the door. Mia rushes forward, opening it, and I toss the bitch out onto the landing for the steps.

"Now leave before I decide to kick your ass," I say in a deadly tone.

"Kick her ass," the man yells.

She looks past my shoulders and then back at me. "The dresses."

"Fuck the dresses. Now leave," I say, stepping towards her. She turns and runs down the steps, and I slam the door.

When I turn, Blaze, Mia, Nonno, and Pop try to hide their laughter.

"You have your Nonna's temper, Piccola," (little one) Nonno says, and I grin.

"She would do anything to help anyone but disrespect her or her family, and she would kick your ass," I say. Then it hits me. I wish she were here.

Nonno's expression matches mine. We both miss her.

Blaze wraps his arms around me, and I lean my head on his chest.

"She's here in spirit," he says, stroking my hair and I nod.

"Go get showered, and we'll find a dress," Mia says, stroking my arm.

I lift my head and smile at Blaze. "See you at the altar."

Two hours later, Mia and I are showered now, and I have her sitting in a dining room chair while I add curls to her hair.

"This is so nice, Gia. I always wanted a sister," she says, and I pause, removing the curling iron from her hair.

I kiss the top of her head, then pick up the hairbrush to soften the curls in her long hair. "You have been my sister for years. You just didn't know it," I tell her.

She goes quiet, and I know Mia has something on her mind. "What's going on?" I ask her.

"I don't want to ruin your day by talking about my problems," she says, and that pisses me off.

I walk around so I'm facing her. "You can always talk to me, now spill."

Mia sighs, and then I see the confusion on her face. "I know Cowboy is attracted to me. The way he looks at me sometimes, it's like he wants to pick me up and run off into the sunset or something. But most days, he's growling and rude. He talks down to me like I'm stupid half the time or like I can't do anything. Then he is mean to anyone else who talks to me. What the hell is wrong with him?"

I pull out the chair next to her and sit. "Mia, you're right. He is attracted to you but fighting it for some reason. I don't think he is intentionally hurting you, but you need to tell him to stop so he knows he is. As far as him being mean to the other guys for talking or hanging out with you," I pause, grinning. "He's jealous."

Mia scrunches her nose up and looks thoughtful; then, a sly smile spreads on her lips. "There is only one other guy that he needs to worry about."

167

My eyes go wide. "Is there someone else you're attracted to?" I ask her, and she nods.

"Who?" I ask.

"Kane and I have been talking and hanging out since the night he took care of me. He's smart and hot as hell, too," Mia says, her face blushing.

"So, you're attracted to both of them?" I ask with a smile, and she nods, but her face looks sad.

I reach forward, taking her hand. "What is it?"

"This is your day," Mia says, squeezing my hand and smiling. "Let's pick our dresses now and get ready," she says, changing the subject.

I don't like it, and we will be talking more later. But I nod, standing.

An hour later, Bo loaded us into Nonno's SUV, which he had borrowed, and drove us to the clubhouse for the wedding. "You two look beautiful. I'm going to have to beat the guys off you, Mia," Bo says, looking in the rearview mirror to see us.

Mia's face flushes, but she thanks him.

We pull up out front and Bo Parks. "Pop has Bo out back in the tent, so he can't see you, and Nonno is waiting in the Lobby...I mean living room for you," Bo corrects himself.

We get out of the SUV walking inside. I spot Nonno and Sammy talking by our new bar and walk over with Mia and Bo.

They both turn, looking me over from head to toe.

"You look beautiful, Piccola," Nonno says as he takes in my satin emerald green off-the-shoulder gown. It has a corset-style top with a long slit up one side and off-the-shoulder straps. When his eyes finally get to my feet, his face contorts, seeing I'm wearing my biker boots with it, and he shakes his head in disapproval.

"I'm just being me, Nonno," I say, laughing. I've never worn heels before and don't intend to start today.

The music starts, and I look over to Mia, who's wearing a royal blue cocktail dress with biker boots. Mia smiles at me, and Sammy takes her arm, escorting her out first, going down the makeshift aisle to stand at the front as my maid of honor.

I peek out through the back window seeing Cowboy standing next to Blaze, clenching his fists, and he can't keep his eyes off Mia. Blaze elbows him in the side, and I laugh.

My eyes roam the crowd of bikers and capos along with their families until I spot Kane. He is sitting in the front row with the Outcast officers, but his eyes are glued to Mia. So, he wants her too, I smirk. My eyes go back to Blaze, who is now turned, staring at the door, waiting for me to make my entrance.

I stand straight and turn to Nonno. He takes my hand, placing it in the crook of his arm, and looks down at me lovingly. "You are a beautiful bride, Piccola. I'm so proud of you."

"Ti amo," (I love you) I choke out, trying not to cry.

Nonno escorts me out the door and down the aisle. With every step, excitement fills me. My eyes never leave Blaze's as he stands before the preacher waiting for me.

His body looks like he is ready to charge forward to come and get me if we don't hurry up. When we reach him, Nonno places my hand in Blazes. I watch as the two men exchange a knowing look. It hits me that in Nonno's eyes, I'm now Blazes to care for and protect. As a former Don, Nonno will expect him to do that. They nod at each other, and Nonno sits as I stare into my amazing man's eyes—the love of my life.

I hear the preacher's voice ring out. "I have been informed that the bride and groom won't exchange traditional wedding rings today; instead, they have chosen to tattoo them permanently after the ceremony.

I hear several chuckles from the guests and some murmuring, but I ignore it. My eyes are solely on Blaze's and his on mine.

The preacher begins reciting the vows for us to repeat, and I squeeze Blaze's hands as the words leave his mouth. When it's my turn, he pulls me tight to his chest, and I have to tilt my head back to see into his eyes as I say them.

As soon as the last word leaves my mouth, Blaze wraps me tightly in his arms, dipping me low and kissing me passionately. I hear whistles, cheers, and hoots from everyone, but I am lost in Blaze.

When he pulls me back up it takes a minute for me to catch my breath. As soon as I do, Cowboy is standing beside us with a broad smile holding a white box up for Blaze.

Blaze gives Cowboy a chin lift in thanks while lifting the lid. Inside is a leather cut. Blaze pulls it out, holding it up for me. His expression is full of pride as I look down at it. Outcasts MC Property of Blaze. Warmth fills me as I turn with a smile so Blaze can put it on me.

After the ceremony, Blaze and I walk together to a makeshift tattoo area where a tattoo artist awaits us.

Blaze goes first, anxious to get his done. I am in awe when it's finished. An intricate wedding band is woven around his ring finger.

An hour later, mine is finished, and we walk around hand in hand, talking to the guests who are drinking, dancing, and having a good time.

Suddenly, loud yelling catches everyone's attention. I spin towards the sound, seeing Mia standing beside the buffet table, screaming at Cowboy to get away and leave her alone. "I'm tired of your head games," she yells, and I see Kane charging towards them.

This can't be good. Blaze and I take off in their direction. Blaze has to separate Kane and Cowboy.

I take Mia, leading her into the clubhouse to talk privately. Bo comes rushing towards us and takes Mia's other hand. We make it inside, and I lead them to my office. Since I know office furniture is there, we can all sit and talk. Bo shuts the door behind us, and we take seats, but I don't release Mia's hand. She needs our support when she's upset.

Seeing tears in her eyes again is breaking my heart.

Chapter 22

Blaze

By the time I reach Cowboy and Kane, they are preparing to kill each other. I grab each of them by their cuts, separating them.

"What the fuck is going on?" I demand. This is my damn wedding. We're supposed to be partying and having a good time, not trying to kill each other.

Kane's head jerks to Cowboy with an accusing look. "Speak up," I order, looking between them.

"Look, I was standing here talking to Mia when a prospect came over with beers. I didn't want to be interrupted, and he and I had words. Mia took it the wrong way and went ballistic, saying I was playing head games with her. Then she told me to stay away from her. That's it," Cowboy growled, running his hand over his face.

"It's because one minute you're nice to her, and the next you're an asshole. Now you're chasing off anyone who wants to talk to her or hang out," Kane says, stepping up to Cowboy squaring himself for a fight.

I pull Kane back and step between them. "Look, I don't want in the middle of your personal shit. So, sort it out and stop trying to ruin my day," I say, staring at Cowboy. He nods and clenches his jaw before turning and walking away.

I sigh in frustration, not knowing what the hell is going on with him. When I turn, Kane is staring at the ground between us. "What's up with you?"

Kane's eyes meet mine, showing nothing but determination. "I think he's finally blown his shot with Mia. As soon as I know for sure, I'm claiming her."

Well, shit, I didn't see that coming. Then it hits me. Mia doesn't turn 18 until next week. I raise an eyebrow and lock eyes with Kane, so he knows how serious I am.

"No one is claiming her until she is of age. Until then, she's off limits to everyone," I state firmly.

Kane lifts his hands in defense. "Shit, pres. no way I would touch a minor. I've kept things respectful while we get to know each other and hang out. It will be nothing but friends until she is of age."

I nod, knowing all my brothers respect women and wouldn't cross that line. But there is much more to this. "Mia isn't just some woman you or Cowboy want as your own. This is Gia's family, her sister we're talking about. So be damn sure of what you want before you make a move," I say in a low tone.

I won't have my woman, or her family hurt, even if that means protecting them from my brothers. Kane nods, but the determination in his eyes is still shining bright.

I clap him on the back and walk towards the clubhouse to find my wife.

Walking through the back door, it's quiet except for some muffled voices behind Gia's closed office door. I open it to hear my new wife's concerned voice, and I freeze for a minute.

"What's going on, Mia?" Gia asks.

"He won't stop," Mia says, her eyes blazing with anger. "I'm sick of his games."

Gia nods for her to continue while I shut the door and walk to stand behind Gia.

Mia looks up at me with tear-filled eyes but returns to talking to Gia and Bo. "He threatened a prospect for just bringing me a beer and saying hello. I don't know if it's because he spoke to me or because of the beer," Mia shakes her head.

"Shit, I'll be 18 next week, and this is a special occasion. One beer won't hurt. Besides, he isn't my Padre or boyfriend. He makes that one clear every day. I want him to leave me alone now." Mia's expression shows hurt and exhaustion as if she's just tired of it all.

"He obviously doesn't feel the same about me, so then he at least needs to let me be happy. Make friends or spend time with Kane. But every time he sees Kane or me talking, he goes crazy," Mia says through tears.

"Oh, sweetie," Gia says, leaning forward and embracing her.

Bo runs his hand through his hair. "I'm going to kick his ass."

I bend down, pick Gia up, and pull her back into the chair on my lap so I can hold her. "Nobody's kicking anyone's ass except me," I say, looking right at Bo.

"I just had a chat with Cowboy, and he is taking a walk to get his shit together. I also talked with Kane, which confused me a little," I admit.

Gia turns in my lap sideways to see me but keeps Mia's hand in hers. "There's nothing confusing about it," she says, glancing at Mia for approval to explain things to me, and Mia nods.

"Ok, here goes," Gia says, taking a breath. "The cliff notes version is Mia has the hots for Cowboy and Kane. They both seem to be attracted to her, but Cowboy has his head up his ass for some reason and is being a dick. I think they could all be happy together if it weren't for Cowboy being an asshole most of the time," Gia says with a shrug, and my eyes go wide.

Did she say they could all be together? A chuckle bursts out of me at the thought. "You didn't say what I think you said, right?" I ask.

"Well, why not? Lots of people have polyamorous relationships. I told Bo that's what he needs too," Gia says with a mischievous smile.

"Why would you tell him that?" I asked, surprised by Gia's views, and then it hit me. I don't share. I will kill any man who touches Gia. My arms instinctively tighten around her waist, and she leans on me, laughing.

"Don't worry, Blaze, you are the only man I want. But it would work for them. See, Bo is sexually ambidextrous," Gia says with a laugh, confusing me.

"What does being able to write with both hands have to do with anything?" I ask, and the three of them burst out laughing.

"She has called me that since we were teenagers," Bo says, shaking his head and falling into a chair.

"Hey, it sounded good in my teenage mind. You like men as much as women. So, you need one of each to make a Bo sandwich out of you," she says, holding her hands up, imitating a sandwich being squashed together.

I can't hold it in any longer and laugh with them. Looking over at Mia, I see she is joining in on the fun and drying her tear-stained face. Damn, I can't imagine wanting two people at once. And I sure as fuck wouldn't know how to act if the person, I wanted treated me like shit half the time.

I need to stay out of it as best I can. The shit will sort itself out eventually.

"Are you ok now?" Gia retakes Mia's hand.

"Ya, I just want to return to the apartment now," she says.

I look at Bo because he knows the plans for tonight, and Gia isn't returning to the apartment.

Bo nods in understanding, taking Mia's hand. "Come on, you, we're having a slumber party tonight. Cold beer, pizza, and chocolate."

Mia's face lights up, and they walk out of the office.

"What's going on?" Gia asks, cupping my face and staring into my eyes.

"You, my wife, are going to be very busy tonight," I say with a grin, standing and throwing her over my shoulder in a fireman's carry. I march through the living room to the stairs, taking them two at a time.

I need to claim my new bride. Reaching up, I slap her ass, making her squeal, then laugh as I rub her plump cheek.

My dick is already getting hard as I charge down the hall to our new room. Since the furniture isn't delivered until Monday, I had the guys set up an air mattress and cover it with sleeping bags.

When I throw the door open, I sit Gia on her feet, and she looks around in surprise. The air mattress is in the center of the room with about six sleeping bags all open and spread out on it. Pillows, drinks, snacks, and three large pillar candles are placed at the head of the makeshift bed.

I kick the door closed and bury my fingers in Gia's hair. "The love of my life, my wife, and soon-to-be mother of my children," I say as I lean down, capturing her mouth with mine.

I push my tongue deep, tasting every part of her mouth as I run my hands over her shoulders removing her property cut. I run my hands down the back of her dress, unzipping it while I continue to kiss my new wife.

Releasing her mouth, I watch the dress pool around her feet, revealing the curve of her hips in a pair of provocative lace underwear. My tongue darts out, wetting my lips. "God, you're gorgeous," I whisper.

Taking a step back to take in her figure, I let my eyes drift downward. She watches me with a smile, and when my gaze meets her again, it's hungry, full of unfulfilled desire. Her chest rises and falls unsteady, and a light blush extends down to her chest.

Without a word, I reach out, tracing the line of her collarbone with my fingertips before cupping her right breast in my hand. She gasps as I thumb over her nipple and leans into my touch.

"Tonight... I am going to fuck you until you can't think straight," I tell her firmly as I lead her to our makeshift bed.

She falls onto the sleeping bags with a soft laugh and lays back, watching me as I strip off my cut and shirt. The look in her eyes triggers a surge of heat within me, and a low growl escapes me as I lunge forward, removing her panties and hovering over her.

"I want you so much, Gia," I murmur against the skin of her neck, nipping slightly, sending shivers through her body.

Gia's hand pushes on my shoulder, and she gets a hungry glint in her eyes.

"Roll over," she demands. "Tonight, I'm tasting you."

Oh, hell yes. I hook my arms around her waist, rolling us so she's on top. Gia smiles as I place my hands behind my head and spread my legs wider. If my wife wants to suck my cock, who am I to deny her?

The look of pure desire in her eyes as she positions herself between my legs only fuels my anticipation. I can feel the heat of her hands as her fingertips glide across my stomach, leaving trails of fire in their wake before they dip below the waistband of my jeans.

The sound of the zipper being pulled down is music to my ears, and a hiss escapes my lips as she brushes against the sensitive skin beneath.

Gia doesn't waste any time removing my jeans. Her fingers curl around my length, her firm grip causing burning heat to pool in my stomach.

She shifts forward, but not before shooting me a devilish grin that makes my heart pound in anticipation.

My breath hitches as her lips wrap around me, every lick and suck sending electrifying pleasure coursing through me. I fist my hands in her hair, encouraging her to go deeper, to take more of me into her mouth.

Fuck, her lips feel so good wrapped around me.

Soon enough, the line between control and desire blurs. My hips buck up, seeking more contact, more friction...more Gia. Each sound that falls from her lips only encourages me further; every moan and sigh she gives drives me insane with want.

I watch as Gia pulls back and starts working her hand on my shaft while taking care of the tip with her mouth, driving me into a world of ecstasy I've never known before.

My breathing becomes ragged as I fist her hair. The look in her eyes is one of satisfaction; she revels in the power she has over me as she takes me to the back of her throat, swallowing around me.

"Fuck Gia," I roar out as my balls draw up, and I explode. My vision blurs, but I can feel Gia swallowing and slowly stroking me as I pulse in her mouth, spurting my seed.

Once I come down from my orgasm, I grab her under the arms, lifting her to straddle my face.

Holding onto her hips, I order, "Ride my face. I'm a starving man."

Pulling her sweet wet pussy down onto me, I dive in, licking and tasting her in long, slow drags of my tongue. The scent of her, the taste of her, is intoxicating, sending my senses into a tailspin as I explore every inch of her intimate folds.

Her sharp cry echoes through the room as I delve deeper, sucking on her clit as she grinds against me. Her hands clutch at my hair as she rides me harder and faster, losing herself to the sensations that ripple through her body.

"Blaze, fuck Blaze," she moans out, each word punctuated with ragged breaths. Her hips jerk over my face, and I feel her clench around my tongue.

She's close. So very close.

"Let go, baby," I urge her on, in between licks and nips. "I want to taste you coming."

Her body tenses above mine as she teeters on the edge before she finally gives in to the pleasure building inside her, crying out my name as she climaxes.

I drink in every drop of her sweet release, not wasting a single taste. Her essence washes over my tongue and down my throat as I continue lapping at her tender flesh until her quivering subsides.

Pulling away from her throbbing core and licking my lips clean, I flip us over again so that I'm hovering above Gia.

There's an undeniable sense of satisfaction in seeing Gia catch her breath below me after such a powerful orgasm: flushed cheeks, swollen lips, eyes clouded with lust. It stokes a carnal desire within me.

I lean on one elbow and take my free arm, hooking it behind her knee, raising her leg high, exposing her to me completely.

I notch my once again hard dick at her entrance thrusting forward in one powerful stroke until I'm firmly planted against her womb.

"Blaze," Gia moans, digging her nails into my shoulders while her eyes lock on mine.

The need to have a piece of me growing in her womb, a piece of our love inside her, is all-consuming. I have to breed her.

"Tonight's the night, Gia. Tonight, I put at least one baby in you," I say as I begin driving my shaft into her warm wet pussy.

After one aggressive round of me taking her and two rounds of making sweet love to my wife, we lay back exhausted but satisfied, limbs tangled in a mess of sleeping bags.

This is the best honeymoon I ever imagined.

Chapter 23

Gia

I hang up the phone after speaking with Valerie, or as everyone knows her, Iron Maiden, and grin. Her phone call was unexpected but a welcomed one.

I swivel my office chair around and look out the window. A few minutes of quiet after the week we've had is welcomed.

We moved in Monday a week ago, the same day everything was delivered and set up in the clubhouse.

I sigh, thinking about what a whirlwind it has been. I'll be thankful once we all settle into a routine.

My phone rings again, and I roll my eyes before looking at the screen.

Sal's name flashes on it, and I answer. "Hey, Sal."

"Hello, Gia. I just wanted to let you know we finished installing the gate, so the property around the clubhouse is now secure. We will start fencing around the Underground tomorrow with a crew of 10. I still have a second crew free at the moment. Where do you want them?" he asks, and my brain freezes.

Shit, we have so much to do, and some have equal importance. I would feel better talking to Blaze and the guys to get their input.

"Sal, let me call you back in a few hours after the town meeting."

His deep chuckle confuses me. "You sound more like a Mayor every day."

"Laugh it up. I'll get back to you later," I grin, hitting the end call button.

A knock on the doorframe to my office grabs my attention. I look up to see Mia smiling.

"What's up?" I ask, curious.

She walks in and plops down in a chair. "I drew up a proposal for putting the Outcasts, well, everyone on Freedom's payroll like you asked," Mia says, laying a file on my desk.

I open it while listening to her talk.

I broke it down by job descriptions and national averages of salaries based on those positions.

I nod in understanding while I glance through the list.

"Bo and I also went to Wells City Bank and got a stack of new account applications and signature cards to make payroll easier. Everyone can fill everything out and take it to the bank to set up their accounts if they don't already have one there," she says, and I look up at her.

"That will make payroll easier for me as far as just wiring from the town account into theirs. But Mia," I pause, looking down at this list.

"These averages can't be right. Do people make this little?" I ask.

Mia nods but has a frown. "I was shocked by most of them."

I scan the list again and jerk my head up. "Why don't I see yours on here?" I quirk an eyebrow at her.

Mia's face flushes. "Town manager is 120k," she replies reluctantly, and I nod.

"I'll make my recommendations in the meeting. Thank you for this," I say, holding the list up.

"Did you and Bo set your accounts up and get your debit cards while you were at the bank?" I ask.

"Yep," she replies, getting up and walking towards the door with a sway to her step.

I tilt my head and think about her behavior over the past week. She seems so much happier. Whatever it is, I hope it continues.

Blaze comes in with that sexy smirk and glint in his eyes. My body lights up immediately at seeing him, and I stand.

He takes me into his arms, pulling me tightly against his hard body. "How's my wife's day going so far?" he asks, then dives in for a breathtaking kiss before I can reply.

Blaze holds the back of my neck firmly while his tongue explores my mouth and massages my tongue. When he pulls away, I have to gasp for air.

"Great now," I breathe out, and he chuckles.

"What's that?" he asks, pointing to the file, stack of applications, and signature cards.

"Things I asked Mia to put together for the meeting. We have a lot to go over and vote on," I sigh.

Blaze nods while running his hand through my hair. "We'll tackle everything one day at a time as a team, just like I promised."

His words soothe me. Seeing my dream become a reality is incredible, but it's a lot of work and slow going.

I pick everything we'll need off my desk, and we walk hand in hand to church for our first Monday morning town meeting.

Once all the officers of the Outcasts take their seats, Blaze slams the gavel down on the new beautifully carved table we all sit around. After calling our first town meeting to order, he pulls my chair up against his, making me grin.

Looking around the room at everyone, Blaze begins. "We have a lot of new business to discuss and vote on today, as we all expected. Gia is going to speak first, covering everything for the town before we start on club business," he says, then looks at me and nods.

"I'll try to be as brief as possible and still cover everything," I say, laying everything in my arms on the table. I pushed the stack of papers to the center that was on top.

"First, those are applications and signature cards for new bank accounts at Wells City Bank. Everyone, including prospects, needs to fill those out and get them to the bank before Thursday because I will be doing payroll every week starting this Friday," I look around the room, seeing their understanding, so I continue.

"A couple of people have too much on their plate. Mainly Mia and Bo."

Immediately, Hawk leans forward with a confused look. "I'm helping him with the underground, so what do you mean?"

I meet his eyes and explain.

"Bo is responsible for more than just the Underground. I have officially given him the title of Gaming Manager, but he is also the town treasurer. With the responsibility of the town's main income source going forward plus handling town funds, it's a lot," Hawk starts to interrupt me, but I hold my hand up to wait a second.

"My proposal is for you to equally share those duties, thereby giving you equal pay for the responsibility," I finish, and Hawk grins.

"I'm game," he says, and I know the pun was intended. So do the guys, as they all laugh.

"Ok, next is Mia. As town manager overseeing all the new projects to renovate the town, she can't handle background checks and the added security measures I want in places for new residents. So, I have a proposal," I say with a smirk, looking towards Hunter.

He is calmly sitting in his wheelchair, listening, but when all eyes go to him, he narrows his eyes at me.

"Blaze told me you are a genius with computers and intel. Is that true?" I ask.

Hunter nods, and his eyes flicker from Blaze to me. "Always had a way with technology, so I went through additional intelligence and counterintelligence expert training," he says with pride.

"Good, how would you like the job of security and tech expert taking over those duties for us?" I ask with a grin, knowing he would be perfect for it.

Hunter sits up straight, and a spark lights up behind his eyes. "I'll need some equipment and an office."

"Make a list of anything you need and give it to Hawk or Bo. They'll take care of it," I say.

I look down at the list of positions and salaries, sighing. "Mia put together some information for me, and we need to vote." I lift the sheet and scan it before I continue.

"The following positions are being filled and what national averages pay. I'll say I want to increase every one of them. So, I'm just going to state the amount I think they should be," I look around the room, seeing I have everyone's full attention talking about money that affects them, and I smirk.

"Sheriff 200k, police officers 60k each times seven people is 420k per year, Gaming Manager 200k times two is 400k, Security/Tech expert 100K, Town Manager 150K for a total of 1,270,000 yearly salaries. Also, I understand that prospects don't get paid until patched in as full members by the club. However, if they are doing extra work for the town, they should. Two thousand a week for doing patrols, guard duty at the gate, and assisting with any building improvements for the town," I conclude, covering everything and handing the paperwork to Blaze.

He looks over the list in deep thought, then passes it to Cowboy. Each member of the Outcast is quiet as they think over what I proposed while studying the list.

I lean my head on Blaze, feeling tired already, and rest my hand on his warm thigh. When he wraps his arm around me, I relax into his embrace.

I listen quietly as they discuss everything and then vote in favor of my salary suggestions.

"You are starting everyone's pay this Friday?" Cowboy asks, leaning his elbows on the table.

I reluctantly sit up straight off of Blaze. "Yes, so ensure everyone gets their account details to me by Thursday. One other thing," I say, almost forgetting, and everyone looks at me curiously.

"With everything going on and the Diablo situation, I think we need to put a tracking or family-like app on everyone's phones. So, we can find each other if something happens. Voluntary basis, of course," I suggest, and the room erupts into chatter.

I knew this would be a major topic of discussion and could cause arguments, but it's needed. We need to take every measure possible to protect ourselves.

Every member of the Outcasts MC is highly trained, but that doesn't make them invincible.

They finally calm down some and decide to table talking about it later. None of them even seemed to consider it an option seriously. Well fuck that, I think. I will speak to Bo and Mia. If it's only us three doing it for safety reasons, then so be it. At least if something happens, we can find each other.

I'm frustrated at how they even responded to discussing it. My mood has changed, and I need to get out of here. I'll decide for myself what buildings or businesses to do next, and they can sort out their own club business.

I gather my things and stand. Everyone stops talking, and Blaze grabs my hand. "We're not finished yet," he says with a confused look.

"I know, but I am. I'll go get things rolling and talk with Mia and Bo," I say, exiting the door.

They may disagree with the tracking idea, but how they argued and tabled it made me feel like they were blowing off an important safety measure. I want everyone in Freedom protected, and that includes us.

Walking into my office, I see Bo sitting behind my desk with his feet up. "Damn, that suits you," I laugh and drop into an armchair with a grunt.

Bo puts his feet down and looks at me closely. "It does, I'll admit, but you need to tell me what's wrong." His voice is firm, leaving no room for argument.

I slide my phone from my pocket, texting Mia to come to my office, then put it away. "Just texted Mia. She'll be here in a second."

Bo's eyes never leave me, but he doesn't push further.

When Mia arrives, I ask her to shut the door. Now, she looks worried and takes a seat.

"Look, it's probably not as big a deal as I'm making it out, but I want to talk to you two. I brought up in the meeting that we needed to put a tracking app on our phones to find everyone if there was ever a problem. Voluntary basis, of course. But it didn't go over well," I say, looking between them.

Bo and Mia stare at each other for a few minutes as if conversing silently. Mia speaks first when her eyes return to me. "I don't see an issue. Especially with what we know about the Diablo's and what they're capable of," she says, pulling her cell phone out and reaching it to me.

I pull mine out and hand them both to Bo. He is much techier than I am.

Bo grins, shaking his head. "I agree. If they don't want to do it, then it's just the three of us again," he says cockily, pulling his phone out and lining them up on my desk.

Bo goes from one phone to another, downloading a family app and linking us. Then he hands ours back. "Now, the three of us can locate each other as long as we have cell phones."

I look at Mia with a stern expression. "Keep it with you always, and I will mine." She nods in understanding, and then I think of her birthday tomorrow and smile.

"Your favorite cake is still chocolate with buttercream frosting, right?" I ask.

She sits straight and gives me a broad smile. "Yes."

"Good, get ready to be thoroughly surprised tomorrow then," Bo teases her knowingly. Damn, he is evil. He knows Mia hates surprises, and him knowing what we are doing while she doesn't is killing her.

Mia stands, stomps over to him, and grins. "Next year, I'm baking your cake with ex-lax as the main ingredient."

I laugh as she spins on her heel, strutting out of my office.

Bo shakes his head and chuckles at her antics.

The door opens again, and Blaze walks in with a blank look when his eyes shift to Bo. I know what's coming. "Can you give us some privacy?" He asks Bo, and out the door, he goes.

I lean back, waiting for it.

"Gia, you can't just storm out of a meeting whenever something doesn't go your way. Sometimes, people need time to think. Especially us, we are planners and thinkers. Well, most of us are," he says, picking me up, sitting down, and pulling me on his lap.

I lean back into him, trying to relax. "Blaze, first off, I didn't storm out. I calmly left. I will try my best to stay calmer in the future, but we are talking about safety here. It's fine, I get it. You guys don't want to be tracked," I shrug.

"Bo, Mia, and I feel differently. We put a tracker on our phones. To each their own, I guess," I say, trying to keep my tone neutral.

Blaze shifts slightly so he can pull his phone out of his jeans and hands it to me, but I don't take it. I stare at him.

"Put the app on my phone so I am connected to you," he says, studying my face.

Seriously?

I turn sideways so I can look him straight in the eyes. "So, you didn't speak up in the meeting saying it was a good idea because you and guys don't even want each other knowing where you're at. Meaning YOU don't want to be tracked. Yet you want to be able to track me?" I say, astounded.

Blaze clenches his jaw in frustration.

"No, thanks I say, pushing his phone away and getting up. Once around my desk, I sit, taking a deep breath.

We sit in silence for a few minutes before Blaze speaks. "Can we talk more about this in a week or two after I've given it more thought?" he asks, and I nod, knowing this isn't over.

"You didn't mention your position or salary in the meeting," Blaze says curiously, and I half wonder if he's changing the subject, but I lean back, sighing.

"By my estimate, which could be off after we finish renovating the town, we'll still have 50 million in the bank drawing interest. I'll still be making more than anyone else in town," I shrug.

"Fuck Gia, I knew that your family was billionaires with the hotels, restaurants, and well...other activities, but damn," Blaze says with a shocked face.

We've never discussed money or personal finances, but I'm glad we are now. I don't want any secrets between us.

I quickly texted Sal, telling him to do the Gym, then the apartment complex next, remembering Valerie's phone call this morning asking about it.

Then I stand, walking to Blaze, holding my hand out. "Come on, let's eat some lunch."

Blaze smiles and takes my hand. As we walk through the main room, I see the man bouncing happily on his perch at seeing me. I smile and walk towards him.

"She's a ho, she's a ho," he says, and I stop in my tracks, jerking my head to a laughing Blaze trying to hide behind his hand covering his mouth.

"Who the hell taught him that?" I ask.

Blaze shakes his head, but his expression is amused. "It's not funny. I don't want him calling me that or any other woman," just as the words leave my mouth, Mia walks in.

"She's a ho, she's a ho," the man sings songs, and Mia gives him an evil look, and then her eyes meet mine.

"We need to hurt the prospects. They have made a bet about who can teach him the most words each day," she says, pointing to the man. "And that's the shit they're teaching him."

Seeing her anger and the man repeating it over and over behind me, I can only scrub my hands down my face.

I not only have a bird that constantly demands we kick each other's asses but now calls women ho's and who knows what else.

The day's frustration mixed with this crazy bird makes me lose it. Laughter, I can't stop. Tears are running down my face, and I'm bent over, holding my stomach.

Soon, Mia joins in, and the room fills with Outcasts looking at us like we're crazy. When I finally control myself, I walk over to Mia, throwing my arm around her shoulder. Leaning close, I whisper in her ear. "Payback is a bitch. If they want to play with the only two women here, we play the game better."

I lean back and watch as Mia's face lights up with excitement. I now have a partner in crime.

Chapter 24

Blaze

Listening to everyone talk around the room, I can't help but pull Gia closer to me and smile. We may all be sitting at different tables in the dining room, but we are one big family now—our family.

I look across the table, and Mia gives Gia a mischievous look. My sexy mi alma stifles a laugh and raises her eyes to meet mine. "Mia and I need to run to the store to pick up a few things. We'll be back in an hour or two," she says.

One look at that face and body language; I know these two are up to something. "Ok, Cowboy and I have that thing to pick up anyway. Take a prospect with you," my voice is low, so Mia doesn't hear."

Gia nods, then looks around the room. "Hey Bo, you up for a ride?" She yells over to him. Bo tilts his head to the side but sits his beer down.

"Ya, let's do it," he replies, standing and walking towards us. Gia kisses me and then jumps up excitedly. What the hell are they doing?

I finish off my beer and then turn to Cowboy. "Let's hit the road," I say as he groans back at me. Neither of us likes riding in a cage, but we have to pick up Mia's surprise.

Cowboy and I ride to Pop's place, borrowing his truck and thanking him before we go to the dealership. Knowing Mia wanted to learn how to ride, Gia had us find her a bike for her birthday.

At first, I was uncomfortable with the thought of spending her money. But after a heated argument over it's ours, not mine, followed by a mind-blowing orgasm, I quickly got the message.

When we pull up at the clubhouse, I park the truck behind it, making sure the bike is covered and out of sight. We walk in the back door just as Gia and Mia enter the front door.

Bo is shaking his head while going straight for the bar. Cowboy and I side-eye each other, wondering what's up, and then I stride toward my wife. "Did you two get what you needed?"

Mia starts laughing, and Gia elbows her. "Go get started upstairs, and I'll be up in a minute," Gia tells her.

Mia grins, taking the bags with her, and I look down at my little troublemaker. "Alright, what are you up to?" I ask.

Gia smiles up at me with an evil glint in her eye. "Your boys messed with the wrong women. We're just gonna teach them a lesson," she says with a hand on her hip. Then, spinning, she marches up the stairs.

I rub the side of my face roughly, squeezing my eyes shut. This is going to end badly. My men, including the prospects, can be brutal. I hope things don't get out of hand.

Looking at the time, I see it's already 8 pm. Shit, we were gone longer than I thought. Screw the bar. I need a hot shower and some lovin' from my woman. Then, some much-needed sleep.

Mia's birthday will be busy, and Pop and Nonno are coming tomorrow.

I enter the bedroom but don't see Gia anywhere. This can't be good. I head for the bathroom, strip, and start the shower. Stepping in, I place my palms on the wall and lean my head forward, letting the hot spray cascade down my shoulders and back, relaxing me.

My eyes open when I feel warm arms wrap around my waist from behind. "I missed you."

"Mmm, I missed you too," Gia says, running a hand over my abs down to my now very erect cock wrapping around it.

My hips jerk forward into her hand. "Fuck Gia," I say as she increases her grip and starts jerking me slowly. This feels amazing, but I don't want her warm little hand.

Grabbing her wrist, I pull it away and turn, pinning her to the wall. "I haven't eaten today," I growl, lowering to one knee and lifting one of her legs over my shoulder.

"Blaze," Gia moans, threading her fingers into my hair.

"Say my name, fuck scream it," I demand as I take that first long lick of heaven. I'll never get enough of her sweet pussy.

"Blaze," she whimpers, her body convulsing under the quick and relentless flick of my tongue. Each moan, each whimper, is music to my ears. Her fingers tangle tighter in my hair as I plunge my tongue deeper into her heat.

"More," she gasps. Her voice is ragged, and I respond eagerly hungrily, feeding off her pleasure and driving her to the brink of insanity.

Suddenly, I feel her tighten around me, and I know she's close. Very close. She's teetering on the very edge, and all it will take is one final push to send her spiraling into ecstasy.

"Blaze!" she screams as I thrust my tongue inside her one last time. This time, though, it's different. More intense.

Her body trembles against me as waves of pleasure ripple through her. My name echoes off the bathroom walls, bouncing back at us.

I continue to lap at her sweetness as she rides out the aftershocks of her climax. There is something incredibly intoxicating about knowing that I'm the one who brought her pleasure.

"Mine," I growl possessively before capturing her lips in a demanding kiss, tasting herself on my tongue. Her arms snake around my neck, pulling me closer. The taste of Gia mixed with desire is pure ecstasy. Yet, it's not enough.

I lift her effortlessly in my arms and step out of the shower, striding toward our bed.

I set Gia on her feet and then spin her around. Placing my hand on her back, she lowers perfectly bent over the bed.

Using my feet, I spread those sexy, long legs, opening up paradise. Taking my aching cock in hand, I line myself up and thrust forward.

She gasps, her tight heat enveloping me, her body accepting mine willingly, which sends a jolt of pleasure racing down my spine. I clasp her hips, pulling her back against me with every thrust. The sound of our wet, heated bodies meeting echoes in the room. Her fists clutch the bedsheet, knuckles white as she pushes herself back to meet my every stroke.

"Fuck..." she moans, and I reach around to circle her clit with my fingers. Her body convulses at the touch, spurring me on to thrust harder, faster. She's so fucking hot and tight that it's almost unbearable.

"Blaze," she cries, her body quivering beneath me, "I... I'm close..."

"Let go for me, Gia," I tell her, my voice hoarse with lust. I move my hand faster on her clit while driving into her from behind, pushing deeper with every stroke.

Suddenly, she cries out my name, and I can feel her climax ripping through her. The walls of her insides clench around me, setting off my own as I pump into her one last time.

My vision blurs as we ride out our orgasms together, everything narrowing down to Gia. Her sobs of pleasure mix with mine as wave after wave of satisfaction crashes over us.

Exhausted yet satisfied, I collapse on top of Gia on the bed, still firmly planted inside.

"I love you, Blaze," she whispers.

"I love you, Gia." I hold my wife tight as we drift off.

We're awoken before dawn by a loud banging on the door. What the hell? I slide out of Gia and put my pants on before swinging the door open.

To my surprise, the hallway is full of angry prospects. "What?" I bello. It better be something urgent to wake me up this early.

"You need to get control of your woman and that one," one says, pointing to Mia's door, which is just opening.

She looks around at everyone sleepily, then a slow smile spreads before closing the door.

"Someone tell me what's going on," I say calmly, rubbing my face, trying to wake up.

"First, they put a bowl of Oreos on the bar last night before bed. We thought it was a nice gesture. But no," he pauses, shaking his head.

They ALL had something in them that made our mouths go numb and taste like shit," he says, shaking his head angrily.

The next one steps forward. "Last night, I took a leak before crashing, and piss went everywhere. Do you have any idea what it's like being drunk as shit and having your piss splash on your legs?" He asked accusingly.

I'm trying my best not to laugh, but I have to ask. "How did that happen?"

A couple of prospects from the back talk over each other, "They put saran wrap over the toilets."

I'm biting my lip now, trying to stay composed as I look at my men. "Anything else?"

"Fuck Ya, all night long, alarm clocks kept going off at different times. Evidently, they bought a bunch of Big Ben's and hid them all over our rooms. Were tired as fuck and pissed," they say, and I can't control it any longer.

I clutch my stomach and laugh harder than I have in a long time. These women are creative; I'll give them that.

Once I straighten and compose myself, I look around the hallway at my exhausted men. "You started this, so you fix it. Now get some coffee and breakfast in you, then start setting up for the party," I say, slamming the door.

When I turn, my troublemaker is sitting in the middle of the bed with her hand clasped over her mouth, trying to stifle laughter. The tears in her eyes are a dead giveaway.

I walk over, scoop her into my arms, and march for the bathroom. "You've started a war, mi alma."

Gia lifted her chin defiantly, and her eyes bore into mine. "One I will win for them messing with us."

The day goes by quickly with all the hustle and bustle of party preparations. The prospects outdid themselves with a BBQ and sides.

193

My officers are carrying out beer coolers while Gia and Cowboy are putting plates and cutlery on next to the buffet as I see Pop and Nanno pulling through the gate.

Those two have been stuck to each other like glue since Mia and I got married. Mia goes to them, hugging each one like she hasn't seen them in years.

"Piccola, you look beautiful today," her Nonno says, smiling warmly as he releases her.

"She is always beautiful," my Pop says, and I have to pull her away from them.

"Enough hogging my wife," I joke, outstretching my hand to shake theirs.

We all eat, drink, talk, and listen to music until it's time for the cake. Gia comes out of the clubhouse carrying a cake, and Bo holds another.

I only knew about the prospects making one. When I glance across the yard, I see them gathering together with smirks, and I know somethings up.

By the time I make it to Gia's side, she is already lighting candles while Bo lights the other. When the singing starts, and Mia walks over smiling, I know it's too late to say anything and stand beside Gia.

Mia blows out the candles, smiling from ear to ear, then chanting starts. "Cut the cake, cut the cake."

Mia picks up the knife, cuts the one in front of Gia, and places a piece on a plate. She picks up the knife again but pauses, looking at the second cake. "You didn't have to make two."

"We didn't," Gia says, tilting her head to the side like she's thinking.

Mia looks at Bo, who shrugs. "When we went in to get the cake, there were two."

Mia turns, looking at the prospects over her shoulder, and cocks an eyebrow.

When she turns back, she raises the knife and stabs it. As soon as the knife enters the cake, there's a loud pop, and the icing goes flying.

It's all over her shirt, in her hair, and on her face. Mia turns bright red, and she growls. It was not a playful growl but one that had her whole body shaking.

She looks down at her icing-covered shirt and the ends of her long hair that now have icing spattered. Mia grabs the hem of her shirt, whips it over her head, and pulls her hair out.

Now standing in jeans and a sports bra, Cowboy and Kane march towards her. Cowboy takes his hat off, trying to cover her cleavage while Kane is trying to block her from sight.

"You think this was funny? Just wait," she yells as they take her into the clubhouse to get cleaned up.

I scrub my hands over my face and then look at Gia, who is furious. I knew this would get out of hand. Gia rounds the table with determination and stomps towards the prospects.

Oh fuck, I start after her with long strides.

To my surprise, she stops before them, pointing her finger. "You think that shit's funny? How many good birthdays do you think she's had in her life that she can remember?" Gia screams at them, and they freeze wide-eyed.

"I'll tell you how many two because you just fucked this one up. You have no idea what she's been through, and you pull this shit. Fix it and clean that up," Gia yells furiously, pointing at the table.

My prospects, grown military men, drop their heads in shame and do what she told them without a word. Shit, Gia's fierce. I wrap my arms around her waist and pull her to me.

"Calm down, mi alma. I think they got the message loud and clear."

Gia leans back into me and mumbles, "I hope so."

It isn't long before Mia, Cowboy, and Kane return outside, and I nod to them to get her first present. It should cheer her up some.

Kane pulls the truck around, and we unload the bike. Mia's face lights up like a Christmas tree at the sight, looking around at us with her hands over her cheeks.

Mia's eyes go from me to Gia. "Is it mine?" she asks hesitantly.

I nod, and Gia steps away from me, embracing her. "Yes, my dear sister, all yours."

Mia laughs and hugs her before going to the bike. She walks around it, running her fingers over every curve.

"There's more," Bo says, holding a box.

When Mia opens it, she finds a matching royal blue helmet and jumps in his arms, hugging him.

Kane and Cowboy step forward with boxes, and Mia eagerly opens them. A leather jacket and riding boots. She now has everything to ride except her motorcycle endorsement on her license.

Gia and I step up beside her. "Now that you have everything, you can learn to ride and take your test," Mia says.

I clear my throat because I have some stipulations. "Stick to the parking lot until you're comfortable. After that, stay in freedom while you practice for your test. There're hardly any cars on the road besides us," I say, but it's more of an order.

Mia smiles eagerly and puts everything on. Once the boots are laced up, a prospect comes over to apologize, but then he screws up by offering to teach her to ride.

Kane and Cowboy spin on him, growling like angry Grizzlies until he retreats with the other prospects. I can't help but chuckle.

Gia wraps her arms around my waist, and I embrace her tightly. We both feel it. We have our family; as crazy as they are, they're still ours.

· · · ·

Kane and Cowboy's story is next.
I can't wait to share it with you.

· · · ·

Click here to follow me on social media and
for up-to-date information on upcoming
books.
<u>authormelpate</u>[1]

---

1. https://www.facebook.com/profile.php?id=61553990836827

Don't miss out!

Visit the website below and you can sign up to receive emails whenever Mel Pate publishes a new book. There's no charge and no obligation.

https://books2read.com/r/B-A-NJQEB-DEGBD

Connecting independent readers to independent writers.

Also by Mel Pate

Outcasts MC
Gia: Outcasts MC Book 1

Standalone
The Fireman Next Door: Firehouse 77 Book 1

Milton Keynes UK
Ingram Content Group UK Ltd.
UKHW020236250424
441687UK00004B/208

9 798224 505302